THE UNDEAD DAY EIGHT

RR HAYWOOD

RR Haywood

THE UNDEAD
DAY EIGHT

rrhaywood.com

CHAPTER ONE

Day Eight

Friday

All around me is death. We stand on the battle field, our small group now greatly diminished and try to absorb the shock of our terrible losses. Tears stream down the faces of Cookey and Nick, making small clean trails down their blackened faces. Blowers looking stony faced and hardened, stares down at the ground. I look over and see Clarence resting his hands on the end of his double bladed axe, mine hangs limply down at my side. I look down the shaft and see the still wet blood, gore and filthy pieces of once human body stuck to the blade. Chris stands resolute as ever, feet planted apart and hands resting on his hips. Only his face betrays the feelings of loss and exhaustion.

I look past them to the mounds of bodies and the now shambling undead still being hacked down. The sight offends me; too much death has taken place here today. Too much suffering. But I know it must be done, and for the first time since this began I let someone else do it. Let them take out their anger and hurt on those rotting walking corpses. As I scan round my gaze comes to rest on Dave who is staring at me intently. The two knives are now tucked back into his waistband and he stands easy, relaxed. His breathing is already back under control, and other than the filth that encrusts him, as it does all of us, he looks the same as ever, apart from the puzzled expression on his face.

'You alright Dave?' I ask him. He nods and turns his head away, but within seconds he glances back and stares again with that puzzled expression.

'What?' I exclaim, shrugging my shoulders.

'Nothing,' He looks quickly away again.

'Dave?' I ask him, something is on his mind, 'what is it?' He looks at me for long seconds, then repeats my actions and shrugs his shoulders.

'Nothing, just tired Mr Howie,' he says finally. That's a lie. Dave doesn't get tired, but I am, I am bone weary and I let it pass. Whatever it is can wait until he's comfortable enough to tell me.

'What now?' Clarence rumbles quietly. I wait for Chris to respond, but he just stares out towards the area where Malcolm fell with Tucker and Curtis.

'Clear the bodies, use those diggers maybe to scoop them up and burn them. Other than that, we need to go after Darren, find where the boats went and bring them back.' I say quietly.

'I don't know what your thoughts are Chris, but after what you did in the commune, I think you're the best one to stay and run this,' I add, looking over at him. He nods back at me, making brief eye contact.

'Okay,' his voice is hoarse and deep.

'Howie, if you want to go after Darren, I'll go after the boats,' Clarence offers, knowing I'll be torn between the two.

'You okay with that?' I ask Dave.

'Yes Mr Howie,' he nods back at me.

'Lads?' I look to Blower's, Cookey and Nick.

'I'm with you,' Blowers says flatly without shifting his gaze from the ground.

'Me too,' Cookey adds.

'Nick?'

'You don't have to ask Mr Howie,' he replies, his tear filled eyes locking onto mine with an intense look in them.

'Okay,' I address them all. Nothing more needs to be said. I turn and stare back towards the still smoking remains of the housing estate, blackened stumps of buildings poking up in irregular shapes.

'We'll find him,' Dave says, giving voice to my thoughts.

'We need to go then,' I say.

'Not now, he's already dead and so will we be if we go anywhere near that estate for a few hours. We'll find him, he'll leave a trail wherever he goes.'

I stare on, in silence.

'Mr Howie, we need to clean ourselves up, take fluids and food and rest, we will find him,' Dave steps forward, clearly intent on making me listen to him.

'Okay,' I say again, it's about all I can manage right now. I look round to see a woman striding towards us. One by one we all turn to stare at her as she crosses the field, stepping over and on the bodies.

'Who is that?' I ask.

'The engineer woman,' Dave replies.

'Kelly?'

'I don't know Mr Howie,' Dave says.

'Yes,' Chris adds.

We stand and watch her walk towards us; her gait is strong and confident. She holds a long bladed machete in her right hand. She watches us watching her and she only stops when she's a few metres away.

'Gentlemen,' she nods towards us. Her voice is strong too. We nod back, nobody speaks.

'Are any of you injured?' She asks, 'Doctor Roberts sent me out to check.' We shake our heads, mumble that we are unhurt.

'Are there many injured?' I ask.

'Many,' she nods, ' they're stacked up.'

'We'll come and help,' I step forward, she doesn't move.

'No you won't, you've done enough. All of you. Go inside and rest, I'll get things underway here. I take it you want them all burned?'

'Yes, but I don't know how we'll do it, dig pits I guess. Or use the deep ditches and whatever fuel we've got left.'

'Thank you Mr Howie, I'll take it from here. Now go inside.' A command, not a request. I look at Chris; he shrugs and starts walking towards the fort. I shrug at Clarence and start to follow him. We walk in silence, stepping over and on the bodies. Taking a detour to avoid the last of the slow moving zombies still being cut down.

We enter the fort and the emptiness and silence greets us like a smack in the face. The fort looks much bigger without all the people inside. Some of the tents and structures are blackened from fire. We walk through the compound, keeping to one side and heading for the planning office.

As we walk further in, I see people sitting, lying and standing in long queues outside the field hospital. The more able bodied go up and down the lines, giving water and words of comfort to the injured. A quick glance tells me most of them have been hurt by their own weapons, or have suffered broken legs and twisted ankles. We pass through them quickly. The whole area goes quiet as we walk through, they stare hard at us. I can't tell what the looks mean, and at this time, I don't care. Someone exits the planning office just as we reach it, glancing at our filthy state before quickly moving away. We pay no heed but walk straight in and see the cold bottles of water left on the table, and the filled buckets on the floor with towels and brushes.

We go for the drinks first, each of us twisting the caps off and taking long noisy gulps, the water spilling down our chins and soaking the front of our clothes. I drain one bottle and go for another; Clarence is already on his third. Dave drinks two bottles then carries one of the buckets outside into the warm sun. He strips down to his undergarments and starts scrubbing at his body with the brushes. We join in, taking a bucket each, pausing only when we realise there are several more buckets left over. The sadness grips quickly and threatens to pull me down into the earth.

We wash in silence, scrubbing the filth from our skin, brushing our hands and arms the most. I realise how much weight I've lost in just one week. My stomach feels flatter, I feel leaner. The result of constant movement and no food. Someone drags a hose out and we take turns to sluice the soap from our bodies in the freezing spray. I drink more water while I wait for my turn; still none of us has spoken since we came back in.

Dave drags the unused buckets out and starts scrubbing his clothes in them, using the brush to attack the dark blood stains. We follow his lead and take the time to scrub our own clothes, wringing and spinning them out. I spin my trousers round and round, watching the glistening water spray off like a Catherine wheel. The clothes are spread out in the sun and eventually we head into the back rooms, slumping into easy chairs, sofas and the few camp beds left in there. I go to the far corner and fall onto one of the camp beds, my mind races for a few seconds, but then there's just blackness, sweet empty blackness.

CHAPTER TWO

That cunt Howie. He thinks he wins again but I won't be beaten. The others have become weak and frail, dropping like flies as the sun grows strong and hot. But I'm not like them, I'm not weak. I know that biting that little prick Jamie will slow them down. They'll stop to cry like babies while I run away. That's the difference between them and me; I won't let feelings get in the way.

We were so close but I should have been better prepared. I won't make that mistake again. I sensed the other hosts becoming weaker; it was like a change within them all. Howie was almost beaten, I saw him go down and I knew I was close to winning, I even held them back from him so I could have the joy of killing him slowly. He was weak and slow and then something happened, he got strong and started fighting back.

The stupid fucking cunt found some hidden reserve of strength; fuck knows where he got it from. Then he rallied them with that prayer. I sent them in stronger, I willed them to fight harder and they did. But the sun was strong and pushing them all day yesterday and all through the night made them weak and their strength just seeped away. Now I know they're being cut down as they stumble about, fuck 'em. A massed attack didn't work so it's time to try something else, and having a fucking zombie army with me will slow me down.

The urge to eat flesh is so fucking powerful. Biting Jamie was the biggest buzz I've ever had, like a thousand orgasms at the same time and knowing Howie and his cunt runt Dave saw it just made it better, even my zombie cock got hard. The taste was unbelievable, and the feeling of his hot fresh blood pumping into my mouth, fuck me. I want more, I want so much more. Flesh won't sustain me though, I need fuel to stay alive otherwise I'll get weak like my poor brothers and sisters out there getting slaughtered. Fuck 'em, stupid cunts.

I run through the estate thinking about the battle. I know exactly where I went wrong, a frontal attack was too much and I left it too long. Cunt runt Dave blew up that fucking estate and then some cunt dug ditches and put sharp spikes down. Then they had guns firing at us but I knew they would run out soon and we still had thousands left. But that prick Howie, he whipped them up and got them ready to fight, I bet he made a stupid speech with stirring words while standing heroically on top of the Saxon, Dave watching him with his little cock standing to attention.

I didn't see many women though, that bitch Sarah wasn't there. I wanted her so badly, so fucking badly. I wanted to bite her fucking tits off while Howie begged me to stop. Fuck it, she must have been in the fort with all the other women and children. No, Howie wouldn't risk it. He expected to lose, I could sense they all did and he wouldn't leave the women and children on their own, undefended, ready and waiting for us to take them. Biting into their succulent flesh and tearing their skin apart. Howie would have sent them away, hidden them somewhere. But there was nowhere left to go.

The urge for flesh is so strong, but I must wait. I'm out of the estate now and running back along the lane. There's houses up here, I'll get in one of them and find food. The thought of eating anything other than human flesh makes my stomach churn but I have to eat.

Where did Howie send them? He must have sent them some-where. Think Smithy...what would Howie do?

I reach the end of the lane, there's a cottage here. The front door is open and I go inside. No-one home, I would smell them if anyone was here. That would be too much to ask wouldn't it, just a little old lady left on her own ready for Smithy to have his lunch. Ha, fuck 'em. In the fridge is cheese and sour milk, butter and vegetables. I need flesh. I open cupboard doors and the pantry, just fucking tins of peaches. Fuck it, I need flesh not fucking peaches. I throw the tin and it smashes through the window into the back garden. Another noise, scampering coming from outside. I open the back door and look down at the fluffy white bunny with giant ears nibbling at the grass.

'Hello my pretty,' I move forward and stroke the fur. Soft and warm, velvety ears and almost blue eyes staring up at me. Fuck it, flesh is flesh and I bite down into the soft back. The rabbit squirms but I bite through the spine and feel the hot blood spurt into my mouth. I lift the warm corpse up and savage at the meat, tearing the flesh off and swallowing it down. It's not the same but it'll do for now and I need fuel to survive.

I drop the corpse and stand up, the warm blood is dribbling from my mouth and I lick my fingers clean. I can still taste Jamie on my hands and I lick them harder, desperate to get the last lingering flavour.

'Where did Howie send the women little white bunny?' The corpse doesn't answer, just lays there bleeding. Something triggers. *White* bunny. The fort's at the water's edge with nowhere left to go. *White* bunny. *White*. I smile. I know where he's sent them. Howie wouldn't keep them anywhere close, oh no, he knows I'd find them. There's only one place left after here. My smile becomes a grin as I walk out of the back garden.

'I need a boat.'

CHAPTER THREE

Waking up quickly, I sit bolt upright with sweat pouring off me. The room smells of farts, and even though we washed before we came in here, it also smells of stale body odour. Blowers and Cookey are still passed out sleeping deeply. Chris is lying on one of the camp beds, flat on his back snoring loudly. I stagger outside to find it's still daylight, I check my watch. It's just gone 1 pm; we slept for a few hours. Dave is sorting the clothes out, folding them into piles.

'Morning Dave,' first words since I woke up and my voice sounds gruff.

'It's afternoon Mr Howie,' he replies.

'I know it's a figure of speech mate.'

'Oh, I always wondered why people said that.' Is he being sarcastic? No way of telling with his flat way of speaking.

'We need to get going,' I say to Dave.

'You, Mr Howie, are relentless,' Clarence says, approaching from the direction of the hospital and carrying several bottles of water in his massive hands. He hands me a bottle, I twist the cap off and drink it down. My mouth feels furry with a metallic taste.

'Where do you think he'll go?' He asks as I tilt the bottle up to my mouth and lean back. I watch the bubbles shooting through the water in the bottle as I gulp it down.

'He'll be somewhere close, he wants to destroy us so he'll be waiting for a chance,' I reply.

'You think so?' Clarence says.

'You saw what he did to Jamie, the look on his face. He was getting off on it.'

'He really doesn't like you does he?' Chris says from the doorway, yawning and stretching his arms out.

'Do you think so? Damn and there's me thinking we were best mates,' I say.

'Anyone been outside yet?' Chris asks.

'Not me,' I reply, Dave shakes his head.

'I didn't go out but I checked in at the hospital. The bodies are being scooped up into piles ready to be burnt,' Clarence says, looking down at the ground.

'What about the bitten ones turning?' Chris asks, scratching his bushy beard.

'They've got a few people out with weapons, taking them out as they come back.' My stomach knots as I think of Tucker and Curtis coming back as one of those, I can see Chris thinking the same about Malcolm.

'What's done is done,' Clarence says with finality, 'we move on.'

'Best get after him then,' I take another swig of the water.

'Why not rest for a bit, if you think he's close then let him come to us. We're safe in here while Clarence goes after the boats,' Chris offers in his normal diplomatic way. The idea is tempting, very tempting. I'm sure Darren won't go far, his hatred for us, well me, is intense and I believe he will do anything he can to get at us. The risk of going out there, with no ammunition left for the guns and only hand weapons left, well it's a big risk.

'We've got no ammunition left,' I give voice to my thoughts.

'Shotguns, we've got loads of them. We didn't use them on the wall, the range was too great,'Clarence replies.

'Sidearms too,' Dave says.

'Sidearms?'

'Handguns, they were no use from the wall either. We've got a few in the Saxon,' Dave explains.'I gave Ted a couple yesterday too.'

'So we're still armed and dangerous then.'

'What do you want to do?' Chris asks, swiftly moving on from my feeble attempt at humour. I look at Dave, but his face, as normal, gives nothing away.

'Coffee, that's what I want to do,' I rub the sleep from my eyes and stretch my aching body.

'I sent Nick to sort it,' Dave says.

'Sort what?' I reply.

'The coffee, Nick's sorting it,' he replies patiently.

'Oh okay, I need a toothbrush too...' my voice trails off, thinking of Tucker and how he'd have a cooked breakfast sizzling away in pans by now, toothbrushes lined up and fresh hot towels probably too. Darren Smith. I swear I'll kill him.

'Kill who?' Dave asks me, I realise I must have said that out loud as Chris and Clarence are both staring at me too.

'Smithy, I swear I'll kill him. This is his fault. The disease or whatever it is, well that happened and everyone had to deal with it. But coming after us like that, targeting us, that was different...'

'That was personal,' Chris adds, a dark look crossing his face.

'I keep wondering if we brought it on ourselves with the amount of them we killed over the last few days,' I say.

'No,' Clarence says with conviction, 'think how many people they've taken. Millions, more than that. There can't be a person left on earth that hasn't been affected by them somehow.'

'They left you alone though,' I retort quickly, thinking back to the commune in London and how little contact they had before we got there.

'Christ Howie, it only happened a couple of days before you

arrived. They would have come for us eventually,' Chris replies almost angrily, 'you're right, this is down to Darren, he did this, or whatever that thing is inside him.'

'Yeah, I guess,' I shake my head and look down at the ground, then realise we're all standing chatting in our under pants. It was only a few days ago that I felt too self-conscious to stand in my parent's kitchen with Dave, just in my pants. How the world moves on.

'Mr Howie, do we have a grievance procedure?' Blowers suddenly asks, walking out of the room to stand squinting in the bright sunshine.

'A what?' I ask, confused.

'A grievance procedure? Under the employment Act any employer must have a grievance procedure. I want to air a grievance,' he explains.

'Fucking what?' I ask him.

'Mr Howie, you left me alone in the bedroom area with Cookey and he tried spooning me...'

'Fuck off Blowers, that's disgusting,' Cookey retorts from just inside the doorway, standing there with his hand in his pants scratching his arse. I burst out laughing with a sudden release.

'This is not funny,' Blowers continues in a serious tone, 'I am more than happy to charge about the country killing zombies and putting myself in constant peril but I draw the line at being sexually harassed in the workplace, there's laws about that kind of thing,' he adds. I shake my head, still laughing.

'Also, and this is a very sensitive thing to inform you of Mr Howie, but er...' Blowers crosses his arms across his body defensively and effects a hurt look on his face, 'Cookey touched me in my private place...' Clarence starts laughing, braying like a donkey with his deep tones, Chris is chuckling away and even Dave smiles.

'Cookey, stop touching Blowers in his private place,' I call out between bursts of laughter.

'Yes Mr Howie, sorry Mr Howie,' Cookey shouts back quick as a flash, 'is there any coffee?'

'Nick's sorting it,' Chris, Dave and I reply at the same time, smiling at each other.

'When this I over, I'm taking you all to an employment tribunal and I'll get millions and be able to retire,' Blowers says with indignation.

'I would be a witness and go halves with you, but I guess I'm complicit,' Chris laughs.

'I, er, don't know what that word means?' Blowers says to more chuckles.

'You thick fucker Blowers,' Cookey calls out from inside the room, still scratching his arse.

'I bet you don't know what it means either,' Blowers shouts back.

'Ah now that's a sight for sore eyes,' I cut in, spying Nick walking back towards us carrying several flasks of coffee.

'Where's the cups?' Blowers asks him.

'Cups? Dave never said anything about cups, just coffee,' Nick says as Dave glances at him sharply.

'Oooh, you've done it now...Dave's gonna kick your arse for that,' Blowers replies with a sharp intake of breath.

'Shit, sorry Dave, I didn't mean that the way it sounded,' Nick says quickly, still somehow managing to make the word Dave sound like the word 'Sarge'.

'There's cups inside, just need swilling out,' Chris disappears into the dark room and returns holding several mugs in his big hands.

'I'm getting dressed,' Blowers says picking up his trousers, 'I'm not standing around Cookey in my underpants.'

'You're a sick fucker Blowers,' Cookey sighs as he walks outside to wait for the coffee.

'Ha, do you remember that bloke on top of the motorway service station,' Nick asks. Blowers and Cookey both burst out laughing as Nick pours the coffee.

'I think he actually shit himself, like proper shit himself,' Cookey says.

'I take it that was something to do with the pair of trousers tied onto the back of the Saxon?' I ask.

'Um, er...maybe?' Blowers replies, the three of them chuckling like old fishwives. I watch them and wonder at their ability to laugh and joke after what we've been through. Their humour is infectious though and it's broken the strained atmosphere.

'Young minds heal quickly,' Chris says looking at me.

'Squaddie humour,' Clarence adds, nodding to himself.

'We were talking before you came out,' I say to the group as we drink the hot coffee, 'We reckon that Darren won't be far. It's clear he wants to get at us anyway he can,' they all stare at me and I almost feel bad for ruining the atmosphere with this serious issue, but it has to be decided now.

'So, we can go out and try to find him, or wait here and see if he comes to us, the fort is strong and he hasn't got an army now. We've got enough people here to put guards up and keep the doors locked. We've still got vehicles to go out and get supplies. Also, there are other forts along the coast, we should try and make contact with them, see if we can rig up some communication between us. The other important thing is to find the women and children and bring them back,' I take a sip of coffee and look at them in turn, inviting them to join in.

'He's got to pay for what he's done,' Blowers says quietly.

'Definitely, without doubt. But he's expecting us to go charging after him now and expose ourselves. We should wait and see if he comes to us,' I reply.

'What if he doesn't, what if he keeps running and gets away?' Cookey asks seriously.

'He's a twisted sick psychopath,' Clarence cuts in, 'he gathered every zombie he could find and brought them here trying to get us, he won't leave it now.'

'Where did the boats go?' Nick asks. I swore I wouldn't tell a soul where they went, just in case but I think these men have proved themselves beyond doubt of their trust.

'The captain was going to try either the forts, the big ones in the sea or take them over to the Isle of Wight,' I explain.

'The Isle of Wight?' Chris replies, 'I forgot about that, I went there on holiday when I was young.'

'Where is it?' Dave asks and I remember that for all his skills and abilities, he knows virtually nothing of normal life and living or much about the country either.

'Across the water, not too far, maybe a few miles.'

'Is there a bridge?' Dave asks.

'No.'

'Tunnel?'

'No, nothing. It's a proper Island. Boat only, they had car ferries running every day,' I explain.

'And a hovercraft, we went over on the hovercraft,' Chris says, clearly reminiscing about his childhood.

'Dave, you alright mate?' he looks suddenly pale and worried.

'I don't like boats,' he says flatly, 'we used them all the time in the service and I hated them,' he adds with a rare display of emotion.

'So you know how to use them then?' Chris asks smiling, and Dave suddenly looks trapped and panicky at the mere suggestion of it.

'Well if he knows how to handle them, best man for the job really,' Clarence chuckles, enjoying seeing the rare sight of Dave looking worried.

'I never said I could handle them,' Dave starts to explain.

'You said you used them all the time,' Chris says quickly.

'Yeah but...' Dave stammers and my mouth almost falls open at the sight of him desperately trying to think of something to say.

'I can handle a boat,' Nick says, coming to Dave's rescue, 'I used to go fishing loads.'

'Okay, so what do you think of staying here and letting Darren come to us?' I put the question out.

'Whatever you think Mr Howie,' Blowers says, Cookey and Nick are both nodding.' Dave sits bolt upright, an intense look on his face.

'He'll go after them,' he says quickly.

'What?' I ask him.

'Darren, he'll go after them. He knows we're too well protected here and he knows we expected to lose so he'll know you would have taken steps to keep them safe. He'll figure it out and go after them.'

'Mate, slow down,' I say, struggling to keep up with his logic but with a sense of panic creeping up inside me.

'Mr Howie, Darren knows we expected to lose. There was no way we could have ever hoped to win with the numbers he threw at us. He knows you Mr Howie. He knows the effort you took to get to Sarah and he'll know you sent them away so they couldn't be taken when we lost the field,' he speaks quickly, forcing his words out.

'Dave, how? How will he know where they went?'

'Howie, he's right,' Clarence says, getting to his feet. I stand up, staring round at their faces. 'There's nowhere else they could have gone, he'll work it out and go after them,' he adds.

They're right. There was no way I would let them hide out anywhere round here. The fort was the safest place for miles and that wasn't even deemed safe enough to keep them. Maybe he'll think they're still here. No, Smithy will know I sent them away. He might be a sick fucker but he's not stupid. He was clever enough to run away when he sensed they were losing. Anyway, there isn't anywhere near here that could hide several hundred people without being noticed. The estate was rigged with explosives traps so we couldn't have got them out through there. The sea is the only place they could have gone.

'Fuck it, fuck and shit,' I spit the words out, angry with myself for sitting here and drinking coffee.

'Mind you, he's still got to find them yet,' Chris offers, once again rubbing his beard as he thinks.

'It's an Island isn't it?' Dave asks.

'Yeah it's not small though, it's got several towns and loads of open places,' I explain.

'If the boats stopped running when the outbreak started, the

Island will be cut off and probably over-run by now. They've only got a few hours head start, if we leave now we might catch them up,' Clarence says quickly, gathering his belongings.

'Nick, you're now the driver, get the Saxon down here and ready to go. Blowers can you go with him and sort out what weapons and ammo we've got left. Chris, did you say there's shotguns here?' I turn and ask him.

'No, I did,' Clarence answers,' Malcolm had them in the armoury. Chris, is there a metal cutter here, we'll get the barrels taken down to make them more manageable.'

'Will that take long?' I ask concerned at anything that could delay us.

'Five minutes Howie, and trust me, it'll be worth it,' Clarence replies.

'I'll get them ready,' Chris starts to move off.

'Chris, I still think you need to stay here, someone needs to run this place. I saw what happens when the wrong people take charge, it needs someone with leadership.' Chris stops and looks first at me, then at Clarence.

'Makes sense Chris,' Clarence offers, 'besides; you're getting too old to run around these days.'

'You cheeky twat,' Chris laughs, 'okay, I'll stay here,' he drops the laugh and stares hard at Clarence, 'make sure you bring her back,' he turns and walks quickly away, heading towards the armoury.

'Bring who back?' I ask Clarence quietly.

'His wife went in the boats,' he replies, staring levelly at me.

'Fucking hell, I had no idea. The woman in the commune who brought us the drinks, that was his wife?'

'Yeah...' I leave Clarence speaking and run after Chris, catching up with him outside the office the police used.

'Chris, I didn't know your wife went in the boats,' I call out, he stops to turn back and face me, shrugging once.

'Mate, I had no idea, I'm so sorry.'

'Sorry for what? It's not your fault,' He says.

'Sorry for not realising, there was just so much going on.'

'Howie it's not your fault, I took steps to protect her and get her away, just like you did with Sarah.'

'But how can you stay here when you know she's out there?'

'Because it needs to be done, and if you, Dave, Clarence and the others can't bring them back, then nobody can.'

'Chris, do you want to go? I can stay here and get the fort up and running again.'

'No, besides it wouldn't be just you staying, it would be Dave too...'

'Dave would go,' I reply with a little confusion as to what he means.

'Howie, Dave would go if you asked him, and then it would be reluctantly, very reluctantly. You and Dave make a good team, there's something special about the way you both operate. Look at what you did just in this last week. I don't think anyone else could have managed that.'

'Don't be daft; you'd have done it the same.'

'I might have tried, but I wouldn't have won the people over like you did. Those young lads respect you Howie. You're a natural leader and like it or not, that's your responsibility to deal with. Yeah, you could stay here and get the fort running and you'd do a good job. But you'll do a better job going after them.' He starts walking off again, I jog to keep up with his big strides and fast pace.

'Chris, you've got years of proper army training and missions and stuff. I don't have that, bloody hell; it's Dave that got me out of most of the messes I got into.' We walk into the armoury and I follow Chris as he starts picking shotguns up from a stack and laying them on a workbench.

'But you put yourself into those situations Howie, when most people would have cowered and hidden away you went forward. We had a saying in the old days, when everyone else runs away, we run towards.'

'Mate, I get that but it's your wife Chris, fair enough my sister is out there but that makes it about even for us, in a manner of speaking. What I'm trying to say is that we've both got the right to go, not just me. We can both get the fort up and running so it shouldn't be just assumed that because I want to go, I should do, fuck...I'm not making sense.'

'It makes perfect sense,' Chris says, quickly checking each weapon and sorting them into piles, 'but what you fail to see Howie, is the way you do things. You and Dave, it's something special. We followed you Howie. Yeah I can lead and I know I'm a good leader, and we shared the responsibility of getting ready for the battle but it was you leading us out there, it was you charging forward on your own.'

'And look at the damage I caused, Tucker, Curtis and Malcolm might still be with us if I hadn't charged off on my own like that...'

'No, we would have taken losses. That is normal Howie. We cannot walk into a fight like that and expect everyone to walk back out of it unscathed...' His voice is firmer, rising in volume.

'Chris, I fucked up. I over extended myself and almost got beaten down. I was fucked and on my knees, if we'd stayed as a group and kept the circle we used before then it might not have happened.'

'If? If? If we had more ammunition, if we had more trained men, if we had fucking planes and tanks...if those things hadn't come after us, there's no room for if's Howie,' Chris shouts, not in anger but trying to make his point. 'And yes, you were on your knees, but what happened then Howie?' He stares straight at me, his intense look unflinching.

'What?'

'What happened then Howie, when you were on your knees?' He speaks low, eyes locked on mine.

'I got back up,' I shrug, uncomfortable now.

'How, how did you get back up. I saw you falter and drop. You had nothing left. I've been in many, many battles and fights Howie, but I have never seen anything like that. You came alive like nothing I've ever seen before. You scared them; something about you scared them and made them hold back. You were surrounded, they could have killed you a hundred times over in the time you were on your knees but they didn't.'

'Yeah, well, just lucky...' I start to say.

'Oh no, not lucky. No ones that lucky. Whatever that was, it was different, special. The whole field responded to you Howie, every person on that field heard your voice and the words you spoke...'

'They were just words, bloody hell Chris...'

'Howie, how many people were on that field?' Chris asks me, his eyes still locked on mine.

'I don't know, we had a few thousand, they had a lot more.'

'So how did they all hear you? With all the fighting, the shouting, people getting hurt and dying, thousands of people all making noise. How did they hear you?'

'I don't know, I was shouting, then you joined in and then the rest joined in. I guess it just carried.' I feel weird, unsettled.

'Howie, we all heard you. Every one of us. It was like your voice was inside our heads or something. It was everywhere.'

'Echo?' I try to joke, I don't like the way this is going. Chris shakes his head, finally breaking his gaze and turning back to the shotguns.

'I've been a soldier all my life, and I've never seen anything like that before, did you not see the way everyone was looking at you when we came back in?'

'They were looking at us, all of us.'

'No Howie, they were looking at you. Even Dave picked up on it. Do you remember him staring at you at the end of the battle? But then I think maybe Dave saw it long before the rest of us did.'

'Fuck off Chris,' I laugh, trying to joke my way out of it again, 'what is this?' He shrugs again.

'Ah, enough said. I'm staying here and that's final. You go and you bring them back. I'll have the fort back up and running in no time,' he turns his back on me, sorting through the shotguns.

'Chris...'

'Time is ticking Howie, Darren might already be after them and you've got my wife to bring back.'

'Okay mate...okay.' There's not much else I can say. I walk out, back into the sunshine and warmth. His words racing and spinning through my mind. I think back to the battle, but to be honest, it feels distant now. It was only a few hours ago and I can remember every part of it, but not the feeling I had. That feels distant, like something I dreamt or that happened a long time ago. I remember going to my knees and feeling weak but then I remembered Sarah and I guess I just found some hidden reserve of strength.

I shrug it off, too weird and uncomfortable to deal with. I look up and realise I've walked the wrong way, going back towards the hospital instead of our area. Everyone is staring at me and I remember what Chris just said.

'Morning,' I call out cheerily, stopping mid stride, knowing I've got to turn round and go back the way I came but I'll look even weirder if I do that.

'Ha, I went the wrong way, what a donut!' I turn and walk back the way I came, my face stinging from the almightily stupid comment I just made. Idiot, bloody idiot.

Walking back, I see the Saxon being driven slowly down the ramp leading from the wall; it reaches the bottom and moves carefully through the camp, coming to a stop just outside our rooms. Dave opens the back doors and climbs in, quickly sorting through the various storage lockers. Blowers and Cookey help lift bags out of the rear doors and onto the ground. Nick comes round from the driver's side and starts opening them up.

'It's a shame to lose the Saxon Mr Howie,' Dave remarks as he opens the canvas bags.

'Well there's a vehicle ferry but I doubt very much if it's running, and besides we haven't booked and it can get pretty busy this time of year,' I reply, watching him remove black handguns from the bags and lay them out on the floor.

'Do we need to book?' Dave asks, 'have you got the number to call?'

'I was joking,' I crouch down and pick one of the handguns up.

'So was I,' Dave remarks flatly, 'have you ever used a handgun before?'

'Oh yeah, all the time.Every day on the ranges at the back of the store.'

'I'll take that as a no then, have any of you used one before?' Dave asks the three lads who are standing watching him. They shake their heads.

'Grab one each, quick run through and we'll practise later. The safety is here, the magazine goes in here. To engage the first round you slide the top back like this...' Dave runs through a lightning fast drill, it seems easy enough.

'There's enough belt holsters there, but only two shoulder holsters.'

'Oh I've got to have a shoulder holster,' Cookey says excitedly, lunging forward to grab one. He stands back up and looks at me.

'Er, did you want it Mr Howie?' He asks with a hopeful look on his face.

'No mate, you crack on, it'll suit you better. Dave who's having the last one?' I see Nick grinning like mad, glancing between Cookey and the rig in Dave's hands, not realising that Blowers has already picked up a belt holster and is fastening it on.

'I think Nick might want it mate, he's almost drooling at the moment. Unless you want it?'

'No, I prefer the belt rig,' he throws it over to Nick who gives a loud shout of "yes" and starts trying to shrug into it.

'You'll be there all day, stand still,' Clarence comes up behind him and starts adjusting the straps, fastening them round his shoulders and showing them both how to fix them on.

'Two magazines each, that's all we've got. Use them as a last resort only. Shotguns and hand weapons first, got it?' Dave gives the instructions clearly. I fasten a belt to my waist and slide the handgun into it.

'We'll leave the Saxon here and use some of these vehicles to find a boat. We can always find something on the other side if we need to. Right, you ready?' They all stare back at me, nodding.

'Get bottles of water from the stores, and get some food to eat on the way. We'll meet in the armoury, five minutes.' We break apart, the three lads heading to the stores area while Dave, Clarence and I walk down to the armoury, entering to find Chris pushing the long barrel of a shotgun sideways through a circular saw, bright red sparks showering high and cascading across the workbench. Clarence nudges my arm and indicates a load of shotguns already shortened. I go over and pick one up, the weight feels a lot different to the big cumbersome things Dave and I used before.

'They're all the same bore that lot, so you can share cartridges. The range is reduced a lot, but the fire power at short range is devastating, which is why gentlemen, they are illegal so don't let any police catch you with 'em,' Chris walks towards us, rubbing the end of the shotgun with some wire gauze, smoothing the end off from the action of the saw.

'Pistols, sawn off shotguns and axes, what more can an elite zombie killing unit need,' I joke, staring at Chris, thankful that he smiles back. The tension from the conversation we had a short time ago is gone. I shrug my rucksack off and push the shotgun inside, the stock poking out the top. I synch the elastic round the shotgun and put the bag back on. Reaching over I can just reach the top of the shotgun. Chris steps forward and tightens the straps, lifting the bag higher on my back. I try again and find I can reach the stock easily. I step away and try drawing it out, the trigger guard catches on the elastic. Chris again steps forward and loosens the elastic slightly.

'Try again,' he says, Clarence and Dave are both watching me, seeing if it will work. I reach back and pull the gun smoothly out of the bag.

'Do it again,' Chris says, helping me guide the shotgun back into the bag. I try several more times, pulling slightly from the left and right, the shotgun slides out easily each time.

'It should be okay, but if you're in a tight spot and it sticks, just ditch the bag, don't stand there fucking about dancing on the spot,' Chris advises me with a smile.

'You know me too well mate that is exactly the sort of thing I would do.' Clarence and Dave both insert their shotguns into bags, Dave reaches his easily enough. But Clarence's massive shoulders prevent him from reaching his arm far enough back.

'You fat fucker,' Chris laughs and I can't imagine anyone else saying that to Clarence and getting away with it.

'Piss off Chris; you're not exactly little yourself.'

'Malcolm was always telling you to stop lifting so many weights,' Chris says, watching Clarence dance about, stretching his arm back but getting nowhere near the stock.

'I should have listened to him,' Clarence rumbles, 'it's not going to work, I'll leave it there though. I've got the sidearm and the axe with me.'

'That's if you can get your fat sausage fingers through the trigger guard,' Chris laughs, then ducks as Clarence launches a dirty rag at him. I smile at the sight and think how similar they are to Blowers and Cookey. The easy banter between them built up over years of living and fighting together.

'We should go,' Dave interrupts, clearly impatient to be off.

'The man's a machine,' Clarence jokes and grins at Dave, who remains stony faced as ever.

Outside we meet up with Nick, Blowers and Cookey. They hand over bottles of water and food items sourced from the stores. They look downbeat and quiet.

'What's up?' I ask.

'The stores,' Blowers replies quietly.

'Tucker did a great job of getting them in order, it felt weird going through it all, knowing he sorted it,' Cookey says.

'Yeah, I know. He was an exceptional man. We've got to go, you ready?' They nod back, still quiet and withdrawn.

We head down through the fort to the first gate, Chris walking with us. There are people milling about, walking around quietly. Most of them still in a daze from everything they've been through. There are men crashed out sleeping, some of them still covered in filth and gore from the battle. A few patrol the top wall, or lean on the parapets, relaxing and staring out with expressionless faces. Chris eyes them all, taking it all in and I can tell he's making mental notes as to what needs doing first.

Reaching the gates, we head through the single walk through one and into the space between the inner and outer wall. We walk down to where the vehicles are stored.

'There's an old minibus van here, big enough for six. Unless you want to take two smaller vehicles?' Chris says. We reach the vehicles and I notice the large plant machinery is gone. The diggers we used to dig the ditches are gone too; they must be outside piling the bodies up ready to be cremated.

'We'll take the van so we can stay together,' I reply. Chris sorts through various keys; each set has been thoughtfully attached to a small label with the make and registration number.

'I bet Sergeant Hopewell got that done,' I remark, 'at least we know they're in good hands.'

'Yep, for now. Any idea where they would have headed to?' Chris asks.

'We'll try the forts on the way; we've pretty much got to go past them. Other than that, no idea. It's quite a big group so we'll look for places that are fortified and can hold large numbers.'

'Are there any of these forts over there?' Chris nods backwards, as though indicating the fort behind him.

'Probably. Must be I guess. The plan was for the whole section of water between Portsmouth and the Island to be covered by defences. We've got this one and others over here and the big things in the sea so there must be some over there.'

'I'd try them first,' Chris says handing over a set of keys. 'That four wheel drive is in the way, I'll shift it if you bring the van out.' I take the keys, leaving the others where they are while Chris moves the other vehicle. The minibus is an old taxi company vehicle, the firm's logo still etched onto the side. Advertising the cheapest rates, airport runs and twenty-four hour cover. The logo makes me think of the planes that would have been in the air at the time it started. Did they land safely?

It's mid-summer and people would be going away for their holidays. I imagine landing in some gorgeous tropical heaven, only to find it infested with zombies and having no way of getting back.

The minibus starts first time, well maintained despite the high mileage illuminated on the dash. I drive forward and pull up just in front of the double gates, now closed and secured after the battle. Two men stand there holding shotguns, watching us with interest. The others take turns to shake Chris's hand and then load in from the big sliding door on the side. Dave goes to take the front, then realising Clarence will struggle to get into a seat, he nods at the big man and gets into the back.

'Good luck,' Chris says, shaking hands.

'You too mate.'

I get in and hear Chris call over to the two men at the gate. They pull the bolts back and start tugging the doors open. I get a flashback of standing here waiting for those doors to open before the battle. I shake my head and drive forward slowly, easing through the gap. I nod at the two men; they're both staring at me. One raises a hand, the other nods.

Then we're out and the scene is amazing. The diggers and plant machinery have been hard at work for several hours under the close supervision of Kelly. Massive piles of bodies have been stacked up in the middle of the flatlands. Far enough away from the fort to try and prevent the smoke drifting back. It reminds me of the body piles Dave made in the supermarket, his was neat and tidy. These are just mounds of human corpses. The men doing the work must know some of the people in those mounds.

The sight is sickening and turns my stomach. So much destruction and death. There are men moving round one of the mounds of bodies, splashing liquid from fuel cans onto the heaps. They move away to a safe distance, someone lights something and throws it into the pile. The fuel ignites quickly and within seconds the mound is engulfed in flames. Thick black smoke billows up into the air. The people on the ground stand and watch the flames.

We drive down the central road, heading towards the estate, or where the estate was before Dave blew it up. The smoke drifts over, the stench hitting us despite the windows being closed. I gag in my throat at the smell of roasting meat and use one hand to cover my mouth and nose. The other's do the same, apart from Dave who just watches it with idle interest.

'That's fucking disgusting,' Nick exclaims his voice muffled by the hand clasped tightly over his mouth.

We drive on as the men carry the fuel cans over to the next pile and start splashing it out again. I speed up, keen to be away before they light the next one. Within a couple of minutes we enter the estate, all of us staring round in wonder. The whole area is blackened, huge pits in the ground show where explosions detonated with the energy forced equally down. Burnt and crisped bodies are everywhere, there must have been hundreds that were incinerated instantly and these came in after. Hardly anything is recognisable. There are twisted melted lumps that could have been vehicles. The houses are just stumps of brick work, random walls poking up here and there. The tyres crunch over glass and debris as we drive through in silence, weaving carefully round the larger obstacles. Towards the centre there is a massive crater and a large void all around it, everything blown away.

'That must have been the fuel truck,' I remark quietly, Dave affirms this with a single quiet "yes". I open the window and poke my head out, the heat is still intense. I guess the stone and brickwork has retained the supercharged heat even from a few hours ago. Again I speed up, worried about the tyres melting, closing the window quickly, the stench of burning stinging my eyes.

'Where are we going to get a boat from?' I call out.

'Head to Portsmouth Mr Howie, there's loads of harbours on the way. Just need to keep to the coastline,' Nick shouts back.

'Righto mate, Portsmouth it is.'

We exit the estate and wait a few minutes before winding the windows down, Blowers pulls the sliding door back to let air flow through. We all breathe deeply; keen to rid our lungs of the foul and noxious fumes we inhaled.

'Does anyone mind if I smoke?' Nick calls out.

'Dirty habit,' Clarence rumbles from the front passenger seat.

'Do you mind then?' Nick asks again.

'No, you carry on. Anything has got to be better than what we just went through,' Clarence turns and smiles at them. In the rear view mirror, I see Blowers, Cookey and Nick shuffling round so they get closer to the open door and window. Dave moves over to give them more space.

'I don't suppose you've got rolling tobacco there have you?' I shout back.

'Yeah, I got some,' Cookey answers, 'do you want one?' He sounds surprised.

'Roll me one please mate,' I shout back.

'I didn't know you smoked Mr Howie,' Blowers says.

'I gave up, then started again, and then gave up. Fuck it; I need something to get rid of that smell.' I watch Cookey laying tobacco into a thin white cigarette paper then deftly rolling it closed, he licks the seam and passes it forward with a lighter.

'Keep it Mr Howie, I've got a few,' Cookey says, sitting back down and lighting his own. I ignite the lighter and for a second watch the tiny flame dancing about, glancing between it and the road ahead. Thinking of the funeral pyres we just saw. I shrug and lean into the flame, sucking through the cigarette until the end glows bright red. I inhale the smoke into my lungs, holding it there for a second before coughing it out, my eyes streaming with tears and hear Clarence's deep chuckle.

I navigate the small roads, keeping to the coast as much as possible. Driving through quiet residential roads that look untouched by the events of the last week. The normality seems to calm our nerves and it's not long before Blowers and Cookey are exchanging abuse, Nick joining in with them. Being this close to the sea, there are signs of maritime interests everywhere. Small sailing yachts and dinghies in front gardens. Signs for chandlers and sail makers. Pubs and cafes with nautical names; The Lobster Pot, The Fishermen's Rest. The area looks well-ordered and expensive. Big houses that only the elite could afford. Not now though. If nothing else, the last week has eradicated the class system. Money has been made instantly worthless and we're back to a base state of being, trade, weapons and who is strong enough to survive.

If mankind survives this event, the world could be a much better place in a few years. Cleaner, safer. But that's a big *if*...and for now I focus on finding a harbour and a boat.

CHAPTER FOUR

That was lucky. Very fucking lucky, fortune favours the brave so they say. Stupid cunts. What do they know about being brave? Fuck all, that's what. I'm the brave one, being hunted to almost extinction by Howie and his bunch of toy soldiers. Cock suckers, all of them. I've been running for ages. I was never this fit before I turned, I feel energised, powerful and strong. That's the little snack I just had, powering me on. Like I said, I was lucky. The rabbit tasted weird but gave me a bit of energy, but I know I need water too. Just the thought of it makes me want to puke but it's got to happen if I'm to stay strong and complete my mission. My mission to fuck Howie over properly.

I found a shop. Just a small convenience store in the middle of fucking No-Where-Ville. I could tell there were people inside; the wooden sheets of ply nailed across the windows gave it away.

I watched from across the street for a short while and saw an upstairs curtain twitch, a face poked out and looked about. The blind fucker didn't see me though. I waited until they went away from the window and ran across. The front door had an awning above it so I got in close, knowing they wouldn't be able to see me from the upstairs windows.

'Hello? Is anyone there?' I knocked and called out, making my voice sound weak and frail.

'Please, please help me,' I knocked again, not too loud though. I didn't want them thinking I was trying to break the door down. Just loud enough to make them think I was trying to be quiet.

'Please, you've got to help. My daughters been injured, we just need some aspirin to get her temperature down, please, oh god please help me.' Fuck me I should get an Oscar for this performance. Noise inside, they're moving about and I can hear low voices. They're discussing whether to help me or not.

'Please, oh please. I don't want to be out here for long. I promised them I would come straight back. The other shops are all looted and empty. We just need some aspirin and clean water.' I give a little sob and knock again. I slump down with my back to the door and my legs stretched out. I know they'll be able to see my feet and know there's just one person. More murmuring from inside, a male and female. I guess from the tones that the female wants to let me in but the male is arguing against her.

'My daughter, she's only five. She's been sick, not bitten but just sick. I promised I would get some medicine. Oh my god why is this happening! I promised her I would get some medicine and sweets,' I break down, sobbing. Well pretending to anyway.

'We'll open the door but no funny business, we're armed in here,' a gruff male voice called out.

'Oh thank you, thank you so much...I've...I've got money.' Bolts are being drawn back, several of them from the sound of it. I lean my arm against the door frame and tuck my head down, covering it with my other hand just in case they see my face. Just in time too, the door opens slowly and squinting through the gaps in my fingers I see a man's face peering at me.

'Oh mate, thank you so much,' I sob again, heaving my chest a little and rubbing my hand over my face.

'You're covered in blood!' The man says suspiciously.

'I know! It's my wife's; she went out first and got bit. I tried to save her but she turned and I had to...I had to...' I heave my chest again for effect, 'I just didn't want Rosie to see...I told her to go back inside but she just kept calling for her mummy.'

'John, open the door and let the poor man in will you!' The female's voice calls out from inside.

'Okay, come in mate. It'll be okay, come inside so I can close this door you poor bugger.'

'Thank-you, oh my god I didn't know what else to do,' I keep rubbing my face and heaving my chest until I cross the threshold and get inside. There are only two of them, both aged in their sixties by the looks of them. The man is holding a cricket bat and the woman a long knife; the silly bitch puts it down on a shelf next to her when she sees me though. Holding her arms out she beckons me to her. So I go. I collapse into her embrace and feel her rubbing my back. I hug her back, and turn so that I face the man. I feel her tense up as I turn her round, then the man sees my face and gasps in shock.

'Edith, let go!' He yells but it's too late. I grin at him and sink my teeth into her neck, biting down hard and tearing into the flesh. The man leaps forward and swings with the bat, I step back and watch him bash his wife round the head. Stupid fucker.

'Oh my god! Edith.' He stares, stupefied, and I grin back at him as we both look down at his now unconscious wife. I chew away for a few seconds, then pick a bit of flesh out of my tooth.

'She's a tough old bird eh John,' I flick the bit of skin on the floor. John raises the bat and goes bright red in the face as he lunges at me taking big swings. I keep stepping back and watch him knocking things of the shelves with the bat.

'Easy now John, you're gonna have a heart attack in a minute,' I step back again as he advances once more, swinging wildly.

'What's up mate, never seen a zombie talk before?' He pulls the bat back for a big swipe, I step in and grip him tight, my face inches from his.

'Come on John, give us a kiss,' I lean in and sink my teeth into his cheek, biting and tearing at the flesh, feeling the hot blood pumping out and spurting into my face. He squirms and thrashes but the fight has gone out of him really. He slumps down and I go for the big vein in his neck. Biting through it and revelling in the glory I pull back and press my hand into his wound, stemming the blood flow. Knowing the infection will congeal the wound quickly I wait for a couple of minutes and let go. The blood pumps out as fast as before.

'Oops, sorry John. I bit you a bit hard.' I leave him to bleed out. At least Edith can join our glorious undead team now.

That was half an hour ago and I've been jogging steadily ever since. It's amazing but just that little bit of blood has given me so much energy. I must be a vampire. Ha, a zombie vampire. Fuck Twilight, I'm a whole new species.

I find a harbour and run in. It's just a small harbour with boats tied up to the floating jetties, fixed in position by solid pylons. I move from boat to boat, until I find one with an engine attached. A wooden fishing boat with a small cabin at the front. I examine the controls and figure out how to start it. The engine splutters a few times but eventually fires up. The ropes are pulled off and I press the lever forward, driving the boat into the one in front. What fucking idiot put it there? Cunts. I get the boat away from the jetty and start moving forward out of the harbour and into open water.

'Little piggies little piggies, where did Howie send his little piggies?'

CHAPTER FIVE

'Any idea's which one?' We're standing round the front of the minibus, looking down at the harbour we found a few miles out from Portsmouth.

'Finding one we can use will be the hard bit,' Nick replies.

'Why, are they like cars with keys and alarms?'

'Some are, the smaller ones just take the outboard off, we might be lucky. This time of year has people going out all the time. All we need is for some rich bastard to have left his engine attached.' Nick explains, his eyes scanning the various boats. He moves forward, the rucksack on his back with the shotgun poking out the top. We must look a right sight, six men walking through a posh harbour carrying axes and shotguns and dressed in military clothing.Nick goes from boat to boat, checking engines.

Clarence seems to have an idea what he's looking for and joins in. The rest of us stand on the pontoon waiting in the warm sunshine. I look down at the gentle waves of the sea, a deep blue colour. The water looks inviting and cool. Small grey fish dart around. White fluffy clouds ride high in the sky and seagulls glide down to land gracefully on the water. The scene is idyllic, beautiful.

I glance at Blowers and Cookey, both of them silent for once, enjoying the relaxing setting. I look towards Dave and burst out laughing at the already green tinge to his face. The noise makes Clarence stand up suddenly from examining an outboard engine. He follows my look and a big grin spreads across his face.

'You look like you're about to puke mate, do you want some water?' I hand a bottle over; he takes it gratefully and starts sipping gently.

'You really don't like boats then.'

'No Mr Howie, I really don't.'

'Oh yes my beauty!' Nick exclaims loudly. He stands up grinning like mad, 'can you believe some fucking idiot left this here.' He clambers out of the black and red coloured rigid inflatable, big oversized inflated frame, seats down the middle behind a central console consisting of a small steering wheel and lever. Two huge shiny engines at the rear, their mean looking propellers out of the water.

'There's a couple of open beer bottles down there,' Nick nods towards the front of the boat, 'I reckon there were people on here when it happened and they legged it.'

'Nice one mate, well done. Has it got fuel?' I ask him.

'Hang on,' he fires the engine up and moves back to lower the two engines so the propellers are in the water, then goes back and checks the dials.

'About three quarters full, mind you these things burn fuel very quickly.'

'It's not that far is it?' Dave asks, suddenly worried.

'No mate, it'll be over in a jiffy,' I re-assure him. The others climb on, leaving Dave standing there looking like a frightened school boy. Eventually he gingerly steps on and takes a middle seat, his hands grasping the hand rail tightly. I dump my belongings next to him and move up front to watch Nick. He examines the instruments for a few minutes, his fingers touching each one in turn. Checking and murmuring to himself. He did this on the bridge in London, taking seconds to figure out a complex set of levers and dials.

'Got it,' he looks up smiling.

'Can we let the ropes go?' Clarence calls out.

'Yes mate, we're ready,' Nick answers him. Cookey and Blowers both take seats. Clarence unties the ropes and comes to stand on the other side of the console, both of us watching Nick. Already the tide has pulled us away from the pontoon and Nick lets the boat drift out before gently pushing the lever forward. The engine rises in pitch, only very slightly and the boat starts moving forward.

'You're going the wrong way Nick,' Cookey shouts out.

'Yes I know,' Nick answers, letting the boat move slowly forward.

'Nick, Nick, You're going the wrong way,' Blowers joins in.

'Fuck off,' Nick shouts back turning the wheel. The boat responds and starts to turn round but the next pontoon is close and Nick pulls the lever backwards.

'Nick, you're going to hit the other boats,' Cookey yells.

'Nick, Nick, you're going backwards Nick,' Blowers shouts, the pair of them laughing.

'Fucking idiots,' Nick mutters, letting the boat reverse slowly, turning the wheel and forcing the nose to face towards the entrance before pushing the lever forwards again.

'Nick, Nick....Nick...' Cookey shouts incessantly.

'What!?'

'You're going really slowly Nick,' he laughs.

'But the right way this time,' Blowers adds. I chuckle at the lads trying to wind Nick up.

'Mr Howie, is Dave holding on tight?' Nick asks quietly. I glance down and see Dave has almost glued his hands to the rails.

'He's gripping for dear life,' I reply.

'In that case, would you and Clarence please do the same,' he smiles evilly and I see Clarence's knuckles go white as he grips the safety bar. Nick eases the boat gently out of the harbour and into the open water.

'Nick, Nick, you're still going really slow,' Cookey shouts out.

'Hold on,' Nick murmurs and pushes the lever forward. The

engines instantly scream out and the front of the boat seems to lift high out of the water. The power is incredible and the boat surges ahead. I look back to see Blowers and Cookey falling off their seats and scrabbling for a hand hold. Nick turns to look and laughs at the sight of them trying to stand up. He waits a second for them to get a hand grip then turns the wheel hard over to the side. The boat lurches over and propels forward, causing Blowers and Cookey to go flying off their seats again.

'Fucking hell Nick,' Blowers shouts out. Nick eases back on the lever and the boat glides to a steady pace.

'What's that?' Nick shouts back.

'That was fucking great,' Cookey laughs, 'do it again.'

'No,' Dave growls and the lads go silent as I chuckle to myself.

'Head for the forts mate,' I point to the two forts out at sea. Both of them are still a few miles out but clearly visible. Positioned either side of the deep channel, marking the route for the thousands of vessels that pass through every year. Nick eases the lever forward, gently increasing the speed until we're going at a decent pace.

The water is calm, like the surface of a pond, and we bounce along with the warm wind blowing in our faces. The noise makes any chance of conversation almost impossible and we travel in silence. I look round in all directions, no other vessels in sight anywhere. The Island looms in the distance, looking green and lush, the ground rising steeply away from the shore line.

'What's that?' Clarence shouts, pointing into the distance.

'It's a pier, connects to the town,' I reply, staring at the long straight black thing stretching out a fair distance into the water.

Nick gradually increases the speed with a gentle nudge of the lever, I keep glancing back at Dave sitting there with his eyes squeezed shut. Blowers and Cookey are both facing into the wind, looks of absolute pleasure on their faces. I try to think of what I know about the Isle of Wight, very little. I know it's big so finding them might not be easy, but that could make it just as hard for Darren to find them too. But, then there's a large group and moving about will attract attention. Especially if the police officers and Sarah are armed.

My musings pass the time until we're close to the first fort, looming up high above us. We circle round a few times staring up at the half grey and half black fortress. It looks derelict with large signs warning the public to stay away. The fort has a mooring point; a metal structure fixed to the side of the building. The gangway leads to a solid looking gate with a heavy padlock and chain attached.

'No-one has been through there recently,' Clarence remarks, standing at the front of the rib and staring at the gate. The waves are more substantial here, the pull of the tide against the fort creating eddies and whirls. Nick fights to keep the boat from being pulled against the fort, making subtle turns with the wheel and the power lever.

'Try the next one mate,' I say to Nick. He nods and pushes the lever forward, powering the boat swiftly past the fort before turning to move across the main shipping channel.

We reach the next one within minutes. This one looks in far better condition with fresh paint on the outside and clear signs of structures running round the top, where-as the previous fort looked flat and featureless. There are windows built into the top section. The mooring point is attached to a more modern looking pulley system and is winched up high; preventing any boats from berthing alongside the smooth walls. We circle round a few times, looking for any signs of habitation or some way of berthing.

A gunshot rings out, a loud retort echoing across the quiet sea. We duck instinctively and I just catch a glimpse of a figure standing way above us on the top of the fort, holding a long barrelled weapon. Dave reacts with lightning speed and whips his pistol out, taking aim at the figure.

'DAVE NO,' I shout before he can fire, 'Nick, back away quickly.' Nick starts moving the boat away from the fort. I raise my arms above my head, hands up. Trying to show we are not a threat. Although six heavily armed men circling their fort in a high powered boat can never look that unthreatening.

'WE'RE GOING, PLEASE DO NOT FIRE,' I shout towards the fort. Clarence has followed suit and is standing with his arms raised, which just serves to accentuate his massive size. A quick glance back and I see Blowers and Cookey have done the same. Dave has raised his arms halfway but I see his holster is unfastened and ready for quick access.

'IF YOU COME CLOSER I WILL FIRE ON YOU,' a loud male voice shouts down, the speaker hidden from view.

'OKAY, WE'LL STAY HERE. WE DON'T WANT TROUBLE. WE'RE LOOKING FOR A LARGE GROUP OF FRIENDS THAT CAME OUT HERE IN BOATS.'

'WHAT?'

'I SAID WE'RE LOOKING FOR SOME MEMBERS OF OUR GROUP THAT CAME OUT THIS WAY IN BOATS,' I try shouting louder but my voice is hoarse and doesn't carry that well.

'I CAN'T HEAR YOU,' his voice is clear and distinct, something to do with him shouting down at us maybe.

'Dave, you shout up mate.'

'**WE ARE LOOKING FOR OUR GROUP THAT CAME OUT ON BOATS EARLY THIS MORNING,**' Dave's voice bellows out and for a split second I imagine zombies in Portsmouth turning to face this direction.

'I SAW THEM BUT THEY ARE NOT HERE, NOW GO AWAY.'

'**WHAT DID YOU SEE?**'

'GO AWAY NOW OR I WILL FIRE.'

'**WHICH WAY DID THEY GO?**'

Another shot rings out, Nick slams the lever forward and we power away quickly. I stare back at the fort and hold my arm up high. Nick raises the speed until we are almost flat out, bouncing along at an incredible speed. He keeps glancing back until he gauges we are at a safe enough distance then powers down to a more comfortable pace.

'Must be on the Island then,' the others at the back don't hear above the roar of the engines. Nick and Clarence both nod back.

'Any idea where?' Nick yells out.

'Head over towards the pier and we'll move along the coast, see if we can find their boats anywhere,' I motion with my hand at the same time. Clarence gives a thumbs up as the boat is turned.

The adrenalin eases off but the incident has left a stark reminder of just how dangerous this world is now, and how desperate people will be to protect what they've got.

CHAPTER SIX

The fucking tide is going out. I can't get the boat close to the shore and end up getting it stuck on a sandbank about half a mile from the beach. I ditch the boat and start wading through the water, it doesn't take long before I'm splashing through ankle deep sea water and then onto the hard compacted sand. There's a big pier off to my right and the long golden beach stretches off far to my left before disappearing round a bend. I had been able to tap into the eyes and ears of my fellow brethren before, but I can't do it now. I was connected to all of them intrinsically, but it feels like the connection has been broken. I keep trying but nothing gets through. Maybe it'll come back when I make contact here; there must be some of my brothers and sisters here somewhere.

'Little piggies little piggies, Smithy is here for you,' singing the words over and over I get to the soft sand and walk towards the high concrete wall running the length of the beach. Howie's little piggies must have left some signs of where they went. Maybe there's another Smithy here, a super zombie like me. Connected to all his own undead like I was. Ha, like a franchise or something. I get the south coast and this fucker would get the Isle of Shite. Fuck him, I'll kill

him and take over. Might be a girl super zombie though. Fuck it; I'll
kill whoever it is. Cunts, dirty fucking cunts trying to make me be a
slave zombie. I'm not a fucking slave zombie, who do they think they
are? Fucking outrageous. It's not right, trying to make me take orders.
I give orders I don't fucking take them. They're dead whoever they
are. They can suck my zombie cock if they think they can rule me.

I step through a gap in the wall and onto the promenade. It looks
nice, clean and fresh. Flower beds and pretty little gardens. The
narrow road seems to loop round a long deep depression in the
ground. I cross the road and see the depression is a lake. Big white
plastic pedalo's shaped like swans are tied up in the middle and shit
loads of real swans swim about. The pond is oval shaped with a
building at one end. I walk towards the building, humming to myself
and watching the swans.

The building has a swimming pool inside. Looking through the
window I see a corpse floating in the water face down. Stupid cunt
must have drowned. Who goes swimming when the zombie apoca-
lypse is upon them? Stupid fucking Isle of Shite people, inbred with
webbed feet probably. I bet the super zombie here is an inbred fuck-
tard too, making all the poor normal zombies do all the work while he
shags his sister. Dirty fucking inbred cunt.

There's no sign of life here. Ha, no sign of life. What did I
expect? A street party? Fuck you. I keep walking along the promenade heading towards the shitty town. The road is bordered on one
side by big houses set back behind long gardens. Probably where they
sat and wanked themselves off at how lucky there were to live here.
Before long I'm near the town, passing a bowling alley and ice rink. I
duck down quickly, seeing a group of figures in the distance. There's
dried and congealed blood all over the place here. Rotting corpses
litter the street. Signs of zombie mayhem everywhere and my little
zombie heart flutters at the promising sight. I move forward,
cautiously flitting between walls and smashed up vehicles until I get
close enough to see the figures are my lovely brothers and sisters all
gathered in front of the front door's to a big hotel. I stay still for a few

minutes and check there are no hero's nearby, wielding axes or trying to be like super golden bollocks Howie. Nothing obvious so I saunter across the road.

The thick fucking idiots don't notice me coming. No wonder they're so easy to kill if they don't take the time or effort to even glance around once in a while. They smell wonderful, rotten, rancid and fetid. I breathe deeply, inhaling the magical aroma and admiring their advanced state of decomposition. They really haven't been taking care of themselves very well. They look hungry the poor blighters. I stand for a few minutes with my arms crossed, they still don't notice me. So I cough politely and watch as they start to shuffle round until they're all facing me.

'Take me to your leader,' I command, half joking but they just stare back at me. Stupid cunts. I try to focus and get into their minds like I did before with my lot. I can't connect though. Some of them are standing at the top of some steps, constantly walking forward into a closed door. I walk up the stairs, pushing them gently away until I reach the door. I push the handle down and pull it open, stupid fucking fuckwits would have stood there for eternity waiting for the magical wall to move out of the way. They groan louder and start shuffling into the lobby of the hotel. Once inside I realise why they were standing outside. The smell of human's is strong here. There are survivors inside. The group stagger forward, heads lolling about and feet shuffling along the floor. For a laugh I act like they do, rolling my head about and pushing drool out of my mouth but it gets boring and I give up within a couple of minutes.

The smell of the humans drives them on and I can't help but get caught up in the moment of the chase. The sense of urgency increases as the scent grows stronger. Body odour both stale and fresh, shit and piss. I can even smell vomit and it's like rose water to my nose. The biggest scent is fear, I can smell their fear. It's mixed in the sweat and leaves a pheromone trail which the zombies pick up on like ants.

The hotel has an old style décor, with dark wood doors and

walls. Old floral wallpaper and gilt picture frames adorn the walls. The horde follow corridors, stopping each time they reach a fire door that opens inwards, too stupid to figure out how to pull the handle. The thing inside me was smart and enabled me to drive my brethren on, I could manipulate and make them love me, make them adore me and I'm frustrated that these moronic shambling creatures are not responding to me. I keep up with them, opening doors and gaining them access to the succulent brains they so desire. This fucking hotel is like a rabbit warren; fucking corridors everywhere. We're like foxes hunting the rabbits down, terrier dogs sent in to flush them out. I ate a little white bunny rabbit a few hours ago. Poor little white bunny hopping about with his long velvety ears and then nasty zombie Smithy comes along and takes a big bitey witey out of him.

The horde stop ahead of me, prevented from moving forward by yet another door. This one has a sign warning of a steep staircase beyond. Ahh, they're hiding in the cellar. The good old fashioned cellar eh, those cheeky little survivors thinking they can tuck themselves away in the dark recesses. Judging by the smell, they must have been down there the whole week, shitting in pots and drinking their own piss. Well they didn't reckon on meeting Smithy the super zombie did they. Cunts. Speaking of which, I turn to the nearest undead.

'Have you got a super zombie in charge round here?' I ask him, he drools back at me with those gorgeous red eyes staring blankly. Poor sod, he looks hungry.

'Come on chum; let's see if we can't get you some lunch eh? I try the handle but the door is locked securely from within. It's a solid door and it will take some effort to batter it down. I clear my throat and knock on the door, three heavy knocks and I smile at the thought of the people inside all shitting themselves and staring up the staircase.

I knock again and start giggling, the zombies round me are groaning and I put my finger to my lips and try to shush them quiet.

'Be quiet or they'll hear us,' I giggle again and knock again, harder this time.

'Hello?' I shout out, 'is anyone there?' No response and I knock again.

'Er hello? Listen I know you're down there. I have some very hungry zombies up here so will you please open up and let us eat your brains....please.' Still no response.

'Listen, we're not going away and we will get in.' I bang my foot against the door repeatedly; the sound echoes round the corridor and shakes the frame.

'Come on! We just want one of you. I can tell you've got a whole group down there. Just send one out and we'll leave you alone.' I press my ear to the door, listening to the low murmur of voices. I start banging my foot again. Steady and rhythmic, knowing it must be scaring the shit out of them. My nose twitches and I scent that we are literally scaring the shit out of at least one of them.

'Just one, come on just send one out. We'll eat him or her really quickly and I promise they won't suffer.' The murmurings intensify; several voices now then the tread of soft footsteps coming up the staircase behind the door. I listen intently as the footsteps get closer until they stop, the person must be standing on the other side of the door now. I pull my foot back, slam it into the door and hear someone jump back.

'Ha, made you jump didn't I?'

'What do you want?' A male voice calls out, a deep voice trying to sound confident and strong.

'Brains...we want brains,' I laugh at myself, 'no but seriously we do need something to eat please. Can you send one out, just an old one. A shitty hotel like this must have been packed with old duffers. Just send the oldest one out, that'll do us.'

'Fuck off mate, there's a few of us down here and we're armed too. Try and get in and see what happens.'

'Hey no need for that aggression is there?'

'You sick fucking...fucking...'

'Fucking what? Sick fucking what?'

'Well you're just sick.'

'Good comeback.'

'Fuck off.'

'No you fuck off.'

'Get fucked.'

'No you get fucked.'

'We're not opening the door and if you try and get in we'll cut you to pieces.'

'No you get cut to pieces.'

'What?'

'That one didn't work very well did it?'

'Not really.'

'Can we try again?'

'Try what?'

'Exchanging insults.'

'Listen mate, just fuck off.'

'Ah thanks, er...no you fuck off.'

'This is stupid, go away.'

'No you're stupid.'

'Do you want them things to find you? You fucking idiot.'

'What things...er...you're the fucking idiot.'

'Stop doing that.'

'Doing what?'

'Repeating things back to me.'

'No you stop repeating things.'

'If you keep making so much noise they'll find you, now piss off and make some noise somewhere else.'

'They already found me.'

'Who did?'

'Those things...the zombies...they already found me. I am one.'

'What!?'

'I am one of those things.'

'Don't be so bloody stupid now piss off before they get you.'

'No, really I am one. Actually, to be honest I'm a super zombie.'

'You bloody dick, piss off.'

'No really I am. These others just stand about drooling but I can speak and think.'

'Oh yeah, and how did that happen then?'

'Well, to cut a long story short; I was a recruit for the territorial army at Salisbury when this happened. We got through the weekend but then this bloke called Howie, and his mate Dave came and sort of rescued us to try and get this big vehicle called a Saxon. We helped them and had a big fight and then went to London to try and rescue his sister. But on the way we got stuck at some services and loads of zombie rats tried getting us. I reckon I got infected then but I'm not too sure on that point. Anyways... we carried on and met this bloke called Chris and his mates Clarence and Malcolm. We went to a hospital to get some things for their commune and then tried to get the sister. Big battle, lots of blood. I got dragged in and turned and McKinney got chomped a bit too. So that's when I became a super zombie and I made all the other zombies be in my army. Saw Howie on Tower Bridge, we shouted at each other a bit; you know... difference of artistic direction, that kind of thing. He said some things, I said some things. I said my army was going to get him, he said his army was going to get all the other zombies. Ended up with us, my zombie army that is, chasing him down to this fort on the coast. But, things didn't quite work out really. Dave, Howie's mate that is, well he set these traps and loads of my zombies got killed. Then there was a big battle and well, if I'm honest about it, I didn't really plan that well and we kind of lost. But I did manage to get a few of his mates killed, er, I think it was Curtis, Tucker and Malcolm, maybe more. Definitely Jamie though, I got him myself. So, long story short I had to leg it figuring that Howie was coming after me, but then I found this rabbit and it made me think of the Isle of Wight and I realised he'd sent them all here.'

'Who sent what here?'

'Oh sorry, I meant Howie; he sent the women and children here.

That's why I'm here; to get them before he does.'

'What? What for?'

'To eat them of course, have you not been listening?'

'You need help.'

'Are you volunteering?'

'Not that kind of help, you need mental help.'

'So, that's where we are now. I'm looking about to try and find them and I saw my brothers and sisters looking hungry so I thought I'd try and help them out.'

'You're nuts. Fucking nuts. Piss off.'

'No you piss off, no hang on; I'm not doing that again. Listen, we will get in and chomp everyone if we have to, or...you can chuck an old one out.'

'It's some lunatic saying he's a super zombie,' the man shouts down the stairs, 'I have told him to piss off.'

This hotel is old, and the cellar would have been used for storing all manner of things in the old days before fridges and freezers. There must be another entrance at street level, so they could take deliveries without having to go through the hotel and scare the old fuckers. I move away and start heading back down the corridor, to my pleasant surprise the horde follow me. I wasn't expecting that. Leading them back through the corridors we reach the front door and go outside, the horde following close behind me. I have to move slowly because of their daytime shuffle.

Outside I spy a set of railings fixed round some concrete steps leading to a wooden door with a small hatch cut into it at head height. I pull the gate open and head down, my horde follow me until we're all crammed into the bottom and backed up on the stairs. I try again to connect to them, so I can send some round to the other door we were just at, but I just can't seem to do it now.

I bang on the door again, call out and wait for a few seconds. The same voice from the other door calls out, telling me to fuck off.

'Open the hatch and you'll see I'm a super zombie.'

'You're a fucking nut is what you....' The man's mouth falls open and his voice trails off as he peers out of the now open hatch. Metal bar's prevent me from lunging at him.

'Hiya!' I lift my hand and wiggle my fingers, smiling in all my dirty undead glory.

'Fuck me...'

'No thanks, I'm not that kind of zombie. Now about that lunch we were discussing.'

'Jesus, you're one of them.'

'Don't call me that, and yes I am one of them, sort of, kind of.'

'But you can speak.'

'Well fuck a duck, look who's being Mr clever clogs.' He stares back open mouthed and turns to say something to the people inside. More faces squeeze into view, peering out at me. I smile and nod politely at them in turn.

'Hi. Hello there. Nice to meet you. How are you today? All the time grinning and wiggling my fingers at them. The first man comes back into view.

'Can you see my horde?' I motion to the side and watch him leaning over to look up the stairs, taking in all the mortified drooling undead. He looks back and nods.

'Good, now we're on the same frequency John...'

'My name isn't John.'

'You look like a John, anyway John, now we're on the same level. How about our deal eh?'

'What deal?' He sounds shocked to the core and the scent of fear has increased rapidly causing my little horde to get all agitated.

'Now now John, we had a deal. You're going to send someone out for us to eat. My little lambs here need some nourishment.'

'I can't....We can't....please.'

'Oh you will John, you will send someone out because you know what the alternative is don't you John? Yes you do. One or all. I will get inside one way or the other; I could burn this door down, or maybe even set fire to the hotel. There's no fire service anymore John, no police and you can swing your knives and weapons about all day long but once we're inside you are all dead, now I will give you a minute to send someone out or we're coming in.'

'Please mate, I can't...'

'Time is ticking John and it's not far from getting dark. You know what happens when it gets dark don't you John.' He nods back, leaning over again to look at the undead around me.

'Please don't do this, please just leave us alone.' His voice is pleading, tears stream down his face. More sobs and crying come from inside.

'Up to you John,' I turn and start going through the pockets of my zombies, pulling out bits of paper and receipts. Eventually I find what I'm looking for.

'Ah, here we are,' I take the lighter and set fire to a piece of paper. It's only small but I drop it down to the bottom of the door and start adding more bits of paper and dried leaves that have gathered in the disused stairwell. Smoke starts billowing out and from the screams inside I know it's going into the cellar.

'Okay, okay,' John who is not John shouts in alarm.

'What's that John?'

'Okay, put it out, put it out,' screams and sobs emanate from inside joined by raised voices, loud and aggressive. 'We'll send someone out,' his voice breaks with emotion. I stamp down on the small flames, quickly extinguishing them.

'That can be started again very quickly John.'

'We'll do it, I swear but if we open this door you'll try and get in,' he's sobbing hard now, not so much the tough guy anymore is he? Stupid fat cunt.

'If we send one out do you promise to leave us alone?' He begs.

'No I don't fucking promise anything you fat turd now send one out or I'll torch this fucking building down and eat you while you're cooking.' The hatch slams shut and I lean forward smiling at the shouting and bedlam going on inside. 'Lunch is almost ready, have you washed your hands? No, oh well,' I smile at my lovelies all watching me expectantly.

'Please, please just move back, we'll send him out now.'

'Roger dodger,' I call back, pushing my beautiful babies back up the stairs, 'come on, come on move back a little.' We get to the top and gather round the railings, staring down into the basement. The hatch opens quickly and John who is not John quickly looks out, I wave down at him and the hatch slams shut at the same time as the door opens. An old man walks quickly out and stands there as the door is slammed shut again.

'Hello,' I smile down at him. He looks up, tall, straight backed and dignified. He looks ancient and weathered but not scared. He looks back at me without fear, staring into my eyes.

'Young man,' he nods once, his voice old but strong.

'So were you forced out or did you volunteer?' He stares back and takes a long withering look at me before he answers.

'I volunteered, I am old and death does not frighten me. Now, let's get this over with shall we?' He starts climbing the stairs slowly, using the handrail. He reaches the top and pauses by the gate, blocked by the zombies standing there salivating messily down their chins.

'Move back, let the man out,' surprisingly the zombies do as bid and move away from the gate shuffling backwards but keeping their gaze fixed on him. The old man steps out from the gate and turns to stare down at me. Bushy eyebrows and wrinkled skin but the eyes are bright and intelligent, I notice his fists clenching.

'There's fight in the old dog,' I smile at him.

'I won't fight you; you'll hurt the others if I don't do as you ordered.'

'If I want them, I'll take them. You fighting back won't make any difference at all.' His eyes stay fixed on mine, a glimmer in them. This old boy wants to go out fighting.

I nod at the zombies surrounding him, I can't connect to them but they seem to understand what I'm telling them. Their groans rise audibly and they shuffle forward, pulling lips back and baring dirty yellowing teeth.

'You filthy fiends,' the man shouts and punches out surprisingly hard for such an old fucker. He connects and sends one flying back. I laugh at the sight and watch as he tries to skip round, punching out with straight jabs. Knocking my lovelies about like a bunch of walking punch bags.

'Go on, get him,' I shout out and they lunge in harder, he keeps punching out, knocking them back.

'Ha, I boxed in the army,' the old man shouts in triumph. I dart in and kick him hard in the back of the knee, he drops down with a loud yelp and I punch him hard to the back of the head, sending him sprawling onto the ground.

'Take him, but not too much. This old fucker might be useful.' I watch in rapture as my lovelies descend. My heart beats faster and I feel a growing sense of excitement as their teeth rip flesh from the backs of his legs and arms. One goes for the neck and I push him away with my foot. He cowers down, crawls back into the feeding pile. I wait for a few seconds until they've each had a bite then order them away. They respond and break apart, shuffling back. I crouch down and hold my face close to an open wound on the back of one of his meaty thighs. The smell of fresh blood makes my mouth pour with saliva. I reach my tongue out, gently touching the wound and savouring the taste. The urge to bite down is almost over-powering but I hold off, torturing myself with the knowledge that I can take that bite if I want to. Seconds pass as I gently lick at the wound, my tongue tingling from the metallic taste of it. It's too much, I can't resist, I bite down and murmur with orgasmic satisfaction as I chew on the still warm, soft meat.

Standing back, we gather in a circle, watching the body. The wound was bleeding openly but within seconds of the infection taking hold the bleeding slows. Then the limbs start to twitch and the body jerks a couple of times. He rolls over onto his back, his legs kicking out in spasm. He sits up and opens his eyes. The red blood-shot eyes of the undead.

'Welcome aboard. Now get up, we've got work to do.'

CHAPTER SEVEN

'Is it a boat?'

'Yes Mr Howie.'

'How the fuck can you see that from this distance Dave?' He shrugs, never taking his eyes from the object berthed on the sand way off in the distance. Fair enough I guess. What else would it be stuck out on the sand like that? But for Dave to actually see it clearly is staggering, the man never ceases to amaze me. The tide has gone out, leaving a vast stretch of sand between the sea and the shoreline. Even the last hundred metres of the sea is too shallow for us to go into without risk of beaching our rib. We've already circled the end of the pier, a massive structure built on pylons embedded into the earth. The pier must be at least half a mile long and is shaped like a hammer with large buildings built onto the T section at the end. There was nothing obvious on the pier, no collection of boats tied up and no signs of life either. We moved off, keeping the shore on our right until we saw the dark object on the sand in the distance.

'It must be his,' Nick mutters quietly now the engine is just ticking over.

'What makes you say that?' Clarence asks.

'The tide has only just gone out, which means the boat was taken in towards the land and beached. Otherwise the boat would be a lot closer to the shore. That boat got stuck there as the tide went out. '

'Makes sense,' I say.

'The sea bed here is smooth sand, once the tide comes back in that boat will re-float and get pulled all over the place, probably into the pier.'

'So that must be either his boat, or someone else that decided to come for a daytrip. What are the chances of that?'

'Not very likely Mr Howie,' Nick replies.

'Okay mate, let's shoot along and see if we can see the other's boats anywhere. It might give an indication where they went.' Nick pushes the lever over and once again the engines roar into life, lifting the front of the boat up. I catch a glimpse of Dave gripping the rails but staring hard at the boat on the sand.

'I'll have to move out in case of sandbanks,' Nick shouts, turning the wheel and angling us away from the shore line a little further. Dave keeps his eyes fixed on the beach, Blowers and Cookey do the same, having ditched the jokes for a while. I should have brought some binoculars.

More haste less speed or something like that. No, more speed less haste. Don't they mean the same thing? I shake my head to clear the confusing thoughts and focus on the beach. A town is built onto a steep hill at the end of the pier, big old Victorian buildings painted white. Church spires and tower tops fixed to the tops of roofs. It does look beautiful and old. Something from long ago, a distant time when things were built for beauty and not just for their practical worth or cost effectiveness.

The town gives way to a large green open area running alongside the golden beach. That in turn ends abruptly at a high wall that towers over the sea. We keep moving on, looking hard for any signs of boats. Another town alongside the shore now, no pier this time though. It looks to be just a small village and I figure the Island will have loads of these all round the coast, which could make our hunt very hard. We follow the coast as it sweeps round a long curve, more beaches bordered by green area's come into view but still no sign of boats.

'HOWIE,' Clarence is shouting and pointing in the distance to another round fort built into the sea, this one looks smaller than the other two and is built a lot closer to the land. I nod at Nick, motioning for him to head that way. He powers on some more, glancing down at the fuel gauge. The boat flies across the water and within minutes we're again circling a fort. This one looks like the first, old and derelict with big signs warning people to stay off and the same style of locked gate. I shake my head and turn to face the others.

'Isn't there a harbour anywhere near here?' Blowers calls out, 'if the tide is out now, it might have been in when they got here. They could have gone right into the harbour....if there is one.' I shrug my shoulders.

'Try back towards the pier; we'll check the other side. We're so far out from shore we can't see a bloody thing.' Nick nods and spins the boat round again, powering on and we slip into silence; drowned out once again by the loud engines.

A few hundred metres from the pier Dave is shielding his eyes from the sun with one hand and waving the other in my direction. I tap Nick on the arm and he instantly pulls the lever back, gliding the boat to a slow pace.

'Over there, looks like masts,' Dave shouts out. I look ahead but can see nothing of any detail from this distance.

'I can't see anything,' I call down.

'There is something there, a wall coming out onto the beach,' Cookey shouts.

'Might be a harbour wall,' Dave adds, keeping his eyes fixed in that direction. Looking round I see that the beached boat isn't that far away. Darren could have been aiming for the harbour when he got cut off by the receding tide.

'We'll go for it here then. Nick, get us in as close as you can and we'll wade in.'

'Got it,' Nick points the boat towards the shore and powers on enough to push us forward until we're in the shallows. The sandy sea bed is clearly visible through the clear water. The boat grinds against the bottom and Nick cuts the engine before moving back to pull it out of the water.

'Have a look for an anchor,' he shouts. We all start mooching about, realising the seats lift up to reveal cupboard space within them.

'Is this it?' Blowers lifts a heavy metal looking thing shaped like a cross, a long rope attached to the end.

'No, that's the flare gun,' Nick replies in a sarcastic tone.

'Alright Captain Blackbeard, keep your hair on. Do I chuck it over then?' Blowers asks.

'Yes mate, it might help,' Nick says, fiddling about with the engine. Blowers chucks the anchor over and Cookey bursts out laughing, causing Nick to spin round and see Blowers going red in the face.

'Fucking idiot didn't tie it on,' Cookey says, still laughing.

'Piss off Cookey, I'm not into seamen like you.'

'Who chucks an anchor over without tying it on first, and you joined the Royal Marines too.'

'Cookey get fucked, and I was only in the Marines for a few weeks.'

'Why? Did you lose their anchor too?'

Dave shakes his head, his bag already on his back. He jumps over into the knee high water and lifts the anchor back into the boat which prompts Cookey to stop laughing but Blowers to start.

'Lost the anchor did I?'

'Yeah well, you still chucked it over without tying it on.' Cookey retorts. Dave ties the rope on and drops the anchor down into the sea again. By that time we're all ready and sliding over the rubber inflated skirt into the warm sea. I scoop water into my hands and wash my face, within seconds the hot sun has dried the water and I feel the tightness on my skin from the drying salt.

It takes several minutes to wade through the shallow water and start crossing the sand and I'm sweating freely already. After the constant noise of the engines, the silence is profound. Looking about I think of the gorgeous weather and how packed this beach would have been before the event happened. It goes on though, the beach is still here and the sea comes in and goes out. The seagulls fly down to snatch at the crabs scuttling about. Life goes on. Maybe we're just one species that has come to a natural end. Maybe that's what happened to the dinosaurs, the giant meteor that wiped them out was carrying a zombie virus that turned them all into undead dinosaurs. That would have been a good film; Jurassic Zombie Park.

We walk close to the boat left on the sand and I can see what Nick meant now. The boat is resting as though dropped by the tide. It wouldn't be like that if it had been floating about for a few days. Someone has been here very recently and Darren is the logical choice. Which means that Dave was right; he is going after the women and children. The thought makes me focus harder and without words being spoken, we all increase our pace.

Dave was right. The wall is part of the harbour, long white masts stand to attention, some with flags hanging limp in the still air. As we get closer we can see that with the tide out, the bottom of the harbour has a thick layer of mud so we skirt round the outside of the harbour wall and walk up through the soft sand and onto the promenade. Finally standing on firm ground with the sun drying our wet trousers each of us, apart from Dave is already hot and sweaty. We walk along the promenade silently, looking all around in case of any undead lurking about, waiting to lunge and bite. None of us trusting that they will be the same slow shuffling daytime zombies that we might expect.

Reaching the harbour entrance we walk along the high outer path and stare down at the myriad of boats and yachts moored up to the pontoons. There are many boats here, of all shapes and sizes and none of us have any idea what vessels they used to transport the members of our group.

'Any ideas which ones they used?' I say quietly.

'Hang on Mr Howie,' Dave replies quietly. He jogs down one of the steep ramps to the pontoons and runs the length of the closest one, back onto the main walkway and up the next one. Half way up the third he drops down to examine something, picks it up and looks about before heading back towards us. He hands over a shiny, metallic object.

'It's a police badge,' Clarence remarks, 'like they have on their hats.'

'Ted! The canny old bugger, he would have left it there on purpose,' I exclaim with a smile.

'So they came in here then?' Blowers asks, looking about as he speaks, 'which way now though?'

'Dave, if you were leading them, where would you take them?' He doesn't hesitate before answering.

'I would have shot that man on the fort and taken that.'

'Okay...Clarence, what would you do?'

'Stay away from the town, it's a big group and very vulnerable. I would head away from denser area's and try to get rural, somewhere defensible where I can hole up for a couple of days at least.'

'Ted was in the services and he's a switched on bloke. Plus they've got the Navy captain with them. I reckon he would do the same thing. So that'll be that way then,' I motion down the beach, away from the town and the pier. Clarence nods back firmly.

'Movement,' Nick mutters, we turn round to see him facing back on the promenade towards a children's fairground built onto a big grassy area.

'Where?' Dave asks.

'In the fairground, a couple of figures moving about.'

'Zombies?'

'Can't tell from here, just saw them flitting between the gaps in the fence.' Nick replies.

'More from the other direction,' Cookey says quietly. I look down the promenade and see a horde moving towards us, unmistakable in their slow jerky movements.

'Ten,' Dave answers before anyone asks.

'Opposite,' Clarence says, more coming from across the grass. A reasonable sized horde clustered together but spreading out.

'I think Smithy has prepared a welcome for us,' Blowers comments under his breath.

'We've got the sea behind us, well a big muddy harbour anyway and zombies on three sides boxing us in. Run or fight? What do you fancy?'

'It's too hot to run anywhere,' Clarence rumbles, 'and besides, they'll only follow us anyway.'

'True, fight it is then. Let's move out from here, I don't fancy scrapping next to these high walls,' I say, looking down at the squidgy mud beneath us.

Walking out of the harbour and onto the grassy area I see more zombies coming from the direction of the fairground, at least another ten.

'Twelve,' Dave says, correcting me as if he knew what I was thinking, which he probably did.

'Fuck me, that makes it about thirty of them and six of us,' I say.

'Thirty three,' Dave says.

'So how many is that each?' I start doing the math in my head.

'Five and a half each,' Dave replies instantly.

'Half each? How are we going to do that then?'

'We could each take our five each and then share the left over's,' Cookey says.

'What's that? Three left over if we take five each?'

'Yes,' Dave says.

'How are we going to share three between six of us?' I ask.

'Take them as pairs?' Nick offers.

'Okay, yeah I like that. Actually, we got three lots coming at us and three pairs, how about a friendly wager between gentlemen?' I say.

'I'm up for that,' Clarence smiles back, the others are smiling and nodding.

'Right, teams? I guess it will be Blowers and Cookey, Nick and Clarence then me and Dave.'

'Not fair,' Blowers replies quickly, 'you've got Dave and Nick's got Clarence and I'm stuck with the bum lord here.'

'Fuck you Blowers, Mr Howie can I swap please?' Cookey says.

'For fuck's sake, Clarence are you okay with Cookey? And Nick you go with Blowers.'

'Still not fair though, Nick remarks, 'you've got Dave so you're bound to win, er no offence Clarence.'

'None taken.' He rumbles.

'Fuck me backwards, okay Dave you're only allowed to use one knife.'

'Okay Mr Howie.'

'No, no knives at all makes it fair,' Cookey says, Clarence is smiling and shaking his head.

'Dave, no knives at all.'

'Really?' Dave asks.

'But, that means Clarence can't use weapons either,' Nick says.

'No hang on, that means you and Blowers get to use weapons, while me and Mr Howie are handicapped with partners just using their hands,' Cookey says, getting a glare from Clarence and Dave at the same time, 'er but that's fine though...' he adds quickly.

'Right, we agreed then? Dave and Clarence no weapons unless they deem it appropriate, in which case the bet is off. First pair back here with all thei r zombies dead is the winner.'

'What about the loser?' Clarence asks.

'Er, the loser has to make the first brew for everyone when we find somewhere suitable, happy?' They nod back in agreement.

'Clarence, if Cookey tries touching you just tell him to stop, he gets a bit touchy feely gropey when he's excited,' Blowers says in mock earnest.

'You're such a twat Blowers,' Cookey says with a long sigh. We break apart, Blowers and Cookey exchanging more insults and abuse as we turn to face our sides. Dave and I walking slowly towards the horde coming across the grass. Dave looks almost sulky.

'What's up with you?' I ask him.

'I like knives,' he replies in a downbeat voice.

'I know mate, it's only for this time. You can use them again next time.'

'Okay Mr Howie.'

'I'll go left, you go right, meet in the middle?' He nods back at me.

'Ready Dave?'

'Yes Mr Howie.' The horde are stretched out in a line and I move over to the far left watching them track me with their eyes. Gripping the axe tight I take no chances in trusting they'll keep to the slow daytime shuffle and move round the back of them. Watching as they start to stagger round to face me. I take the opportunity and move in quickly; striking the first one through the neck and taking his head clean off. I step backwards and check around me, then dart in and sweep the axe down, cleaving into the skull of an undead female, splitting her cranium apart and spilling brains out onto her shoulders before she sags down.

A quick glance and I can see Dave has already taken three down and is on his fourth. Violently wrenching the head sideways to break the neck. I swing the double headed axe into the stomach of the next one, cutting deep into their midriff and watching bright red innards falling out. Punching down into the face as I draw the axe back I turn for the next one to find them all down and Dave standing there watching me.

'I only got three.'

'Sorry, did you want more Mr Howie?'

'Bit late now, unless they come back again as undead undead's.' Turning to check on the others, I see Clarence lifting his last one up bodily before dropping it down hard on his knee, breaking the spine. He rolls the body off his leg and looks over, both of us realising we've each finished and sprinting back to the start at the same time. We both dive forward and land in a heap, laughing and giggling like idiots, trying to push each other away.

'Ah fucking hell,' Blowers moans as he and Nick both look at their last standing zombie, an old man with big bushy eyebrows. 'We've lost,' he adds sorely. The old man undead shuffles closer to Blowers then suddenly darts forward with speed. We shout a warning and Blowers ducks out the way. The old man zombie turns with surprising dexterity and faces Blowers again, before raising his fists in a boxing pose and going at Blowers with a fast pace, throwing straight jabs at Blowers' head.

Blowers ducks and weaves backwards, instinctively raising his own fists to protect his face. He lashes out and the old man blocks the punch, throwing another one which just misses Blowers as he ducks down.

'What's he doing?' Cookey shouts in alarm, watching Blowers trading punches with an ancient zombie boxer.

'He's quick, I'll give him that,' Clarence says, watching the spectacle.

'Who, Blowers or the zombie?' I ask.

'The zombie, he's very quick and he looks fresh too. No decay and the wound on the back of his leg is still open.'

'He's just been turned then,' I say. Dave has drawn his handgun and tracks the zombie darting about and throwing punches at Blowers.

Blowers suddenly speeds up and launches a flurry of body blows on the zombie, sending him reeling backwards. He keeps up the barrage, carefully avoiding hitting the zombie in the face but landing blows everywhere else, including the side of his head with powerful hooks.

'BLOWERS, MOVE BACK,' Dave shouts, still trying to track the zombie with his pistol.

'I've got him,' Blowers shouts back.

'MOVE BACK NOW,' Dave roars, Blowers instantly does as he's told. Dave holsters his weapon and runs towards the zombie, drawing a knife and sweeping it across the old man's throat. He savagely jerks the head back as he does it, forcing the zombie to fall face down on the ground.

'DON'T EVER DO THAT AGAIN,' Dave roars at a stunned Blowers.

'You could cut your hands and get his blood in you, show me your hands.'

'But I thought of that and didn't hit his face,' Blowers replies meekly.

'Show me your hands,' Dave says, his voice still hard edged. Blowers holds his hands out palms down as Dave inspects them closely.

'I'm really sorry Dave,' Blowers says, he looks crest fallen. Any of us would being told off by Dave like that, 'I did avoid hitting his face in case I cut myself.'

'He's already bleeding and we still don't know how Darren got infected,' Dave replies quickly.

'I'm sorry Dave,' Blowers repeats, looking ashamed and embarrassed.

'It's done now,' Dave drops his hands and starts to turn away, 'good moves though, good skills, well done. We'll practise more of that later,' Dave adds in a softer tone. I'm both stunned and amazed at Dave showing awareness of someone else's feelings like that, 'and you're making the brews later.'

This time my mouth drops open.

CHAPTER EIGHT

I've made a connection, that old fucker from the hotel cellar. It must have been the blood I took from him. If I'd known that I would have brought that old crow I bit in the shop with me. I can't see through his eyes but there's definitely a connection there. As soon as he got up off the ground I knew he was mine. It's got to be the blood we shared. I wonder if it works with other bodily fluids or just blood.

Those fucking wanking fucktards, standing over there on the grass chatting all cool and heroic while my lovelies surround them. I only sent a few in, save the rest for later. I've been a busy boy running round this shitty little town collecting up my groupies. Although I can't connect to them, they still follow me. And that old boy, well he's a peach. There's something there, a feeling of control, a bit like before when I had my army only not so strong. I can will him to move and do things but I can't see or hear anything from him. Oh well, make the best of a bad lot I say. But those utter cunts, I fucking hate them. I fucking detest them, I'm going to rip their fucking heads off and unload my zombie runny turds down their throats. No, better than that; I'll tie them down and get my lovelies to hold their mouths open while I shit down their still living throats. Yeah, fuck yeah. Infection by poo. Fuck you Howie, eat my shit.

I stand across the road in some gardens, peering through the bushes like some dirty voyeur. The stupid cunts were racing up and down the sea in a high powered boat, letting every zombie in the town know they're coming. Fucking cock chops, what did they expect? Using a fucking great boat like that and then storming up the beach like a bunch of invading twats.

I blame Dave the nasty little runtcunt. Dave the cuntrunt. Cuntrunt Dave. Now look at them, going off in pairs and taking my babies out. You wait though, you fucking wait for my old boy. Couldn't work out better than Blowers and that thick fucker Nick going over to him. Oh look at Dave snapping necks like a regular Rambo, and Clarence chucking them about like dolls. I can see Howie and my zombie cock twitches with the thought of watching him die right now. Ha, there's my old boy giving it the slow shuffle and waiting for Blowers to get in nice and close.

Fuck me, he was quick, he's throwing punches like a right old brawler. Look at him go, straight for Blowers. One-two, yeah go on smash his fucking teeth in. Blowers is quick though and ducks about smacking my lovely old man about. This is fucking classic, watching Blowers getting ragged about by an old man until Dave shouts and stabs him in the neck. Fucking spoilsport. He ruins everything. He has to fucking take over doesn't he? Now look at him, standing there caressing Blowers hands, probably giving him a sly hand-job at the same time.

'YOU UTTER FUCKING CUNTS,' fuck me, did I just do that. Oops, bit too soon. Oh shit, they heard me; here they come; running like a bunch of girls. I jump out, stick my fingers up and then leg it with billy big legs.

'**I WILL KILL YOU,**' that's Dave roaring away with his big voice. Gotta catch me first you stumpy little midget. I run quickly with the advantage of already scouting the way. Going down the side of the house and running down the street towards the town. Come on you cunts, chase me.

Keep coming you fuckers. I reach the end of the road and stand on the junction for a second until they come into view, Dave out front sprinting hard. I wave and start running again. Leading them down narrow streets and back towards the town. I reach another junction with a steep hill going off to my left and the seafront down to my right. I pause for a second to make sure they can see me and start off up the hill.

There's an old derelict hotel up here that I spied earlier. Perfect for what I've got in mind. The hill is steep but the infection keeps me going, powering me on where-as before I would have collapsed on the ground by now, sucking on a cigarette. Dirty things. Funny that, I haven't wanted one since I turned. Hey, give up smoking and be a zombie! Fuck, Dave is quick. I pause just long enough to make sure they're all coming and I run into the over grown grounds. What was once a large car park is now covered in huge weeds and bushes. I run round the back and open the door I prepared earlier and then run off in the other direction and over the high wall into an adjoining garden. I slump down beneath the wall and get my breathing under control, listening for the footsteps of Dave and his merry men.

'Round here,' Dave bellows out and it's not long before I hear the rest of them chugging into the grounds to join their stumpy little mate.

'Where did he go?' I hear Howie panting.

'I lost him here,' Dave answers.

'That door's open, he must have gone in there,' Howie says.

'Maybe, or he could have gone over that wall or round the other side,' Dave says.

'It'll be dark soon we need to get off the street,' that's Clarence's deep voice.

'Fuck it, he must have gone in there,' Howie says.

'We going in?' Blowers voice.

'Yeah come on,' Howie says. My smile grows wide as I listen to them pushing the door open and entering the hotel. Perfect, fucking perfect. That hotel is huge and it will take them a while to work their way round, plus there are the little surprises I left for them. Poor little babies locked in hotel rooms on their own. Fuck it, might get a lucky bite out of one of them.

I wait another ten minutes until the shadows grow longer and the sky darkens. They'll be well within the building now. Slowly peeking out over the top of the wall, I make sure they have gone inside and not left a trap for me. No sign of them. Good, I climb over and drop down on the other side. I sneak over to the door and pull it closed, there's an old padlock clasp on the door, attached to a loop on the wall. I get the bit of metal I found earlier and jam it into the loop, securing the door closed. Stupid fuckwits. How did they win the battle with stupidity like this?

Running over the road and into a front garden, I work my way to the high wooden gate giving access to the rear garden. Pushing it open I smile at the lovely horde all waiting for me. I leave the gate open and move down a few houses, repeating the action. Only forty or so zombies, not enough and I look into the sky, willing the sun to drop down and let the night begin.

I know what will happen and I feel a sense of excitement course through my wonderfully infected system. The zombies shuffle out of their garden gates and slowly trudge across the road towards the hotel. The last glimmer of sun high on the side of the hotel slowly slides up the wall. Looking down the hill I can see the sea shimmering with golden rays as the sun drops down. Any second now, come on you fucking cunts. My foot is tapping with impatience at the still shuffling zombies, stupid fucking idiots. Why don't they speed up? Don't they know Howie and his gang of zombie bashers are in that hotel?

Fuck yes! Here it is. The sun drops and my lovelies all stand still, lifting their beautiful rotten faces to the sky. The urge overtakes me and I do the same. As one we roar out, letting all the other zombies know where we are. Howling guttural wails fill the air as every undead across the land lifts their head and screams into the night. Fuck you Howie, we're not slow and shuffling now are we? The howling ceases and my beauties come alive, moving faster and with purpose they pour across the road heading for the hotel. I glance up and see pale faces peering out from the grimy windows. They've heard the howling and come to look. One of them must have seen me, he fires through the window and I just about duck down as the round whips by my head.

Fucking lovely, that shot will bring all my brothers and sisters here. Couldn't have been Dave firing, the lack of a new hole in my head tells me that. Groans and scuffles come from all around me as zombies stagger towards the hotel. Moving fast now, their movements more controlled and the evil presence of them intensifies. Love it. Fucking love it.

Now it's nice and dark I keep to the shadows skirting the edge of the building, moving low between windows and glass paned doors. The hotel has balconies on most levels, rising at least five stories up and I keep a close eye on them in case they fire down at me. A large number of my zombies follow me, keeping up easily now it's dark. I lead them to the rear and pull the clasp open, shoving the door open and letting the zombies stagger inside. After about twenty have passed through, I pull the door closed and re-fasten the clasp. Leading more zombies round the side and looking for other entrances. I want to leave groups at the doors and exit points to prevent the fuckers getting out, but there's no control over these zombies and they just follow me about. A full loop round the hotel and I'm back to the door at the rear, leading a huge horde with me. There's loads now, pouring in from all directions; drawn by the noise of the gunshot and activity and the smell of each other. The only way to stop them following me is for me to lose them somehow, but I need to keep them here to trap Howie and his cunts.

Opening the door again I slip inside and let a few more follow me through seeing as there's shit loads of them outside. Once a few more have got in I push the door closed and force some poor zombie to stagger backwards. Wedging a chair under the handle I move off deeper into the hotel. The only light is from the bright moon shining through the windows. I work my way quietly towards the front as my new horde get the smell of humans in their noses and start off into the deep recesses, following the scent trail. An old fire exit marks my way out and I push the big metal handle down, easing the door open and squeezing out. The door locks when I push it closed and I quickly dart across the road, ducking down in the shadows to turn back and watch for a bit.

My lovelies are all round the hotel now, groaning away with hunger as they sense survivors inside. Howie and his bum-chum mates will have a nice surprise. Couldn't have worked out better. Leaving them busy for the night, I move off to continue my search for Howie's little piggies.

CHAPTER NINE

We enter the hotel and work our way through the corridors out into the main lobby by the front doors, now encrusted with grime and filth. This hotel must have been grand once with wide rooms and high ceilings. The main lobby has a huge spiral staircase leading to the upper floors. A smashed up chandelier lies on the floor in the middle of the lobby. Broken glass, smashed plates and crockery cover the carpet. Furniture from the hotel bedrooms has been lobbed down from the upper floors too, adding to the debris.

The décor is old, really 1960's with floral wall paper and a deep red carpet, dark wood and lots of brass fittings everywhere. Staying together we work our way into a long ballroom with wooden floors and stacks of chairs piled up along the sides. An old bar stands at one end, still with some glasses stacked on the shelves. Dave and Clarence both scan the floor, pointing out fresh tread marks distinctive in the dust.

'Someone definitely came through here very recently, looks like they went through here and into the lobby,' Clarence comments, squatting down to look at the marks.

'Upstairs?' I ask him and Dave.

'This place is huge, he could be anywhere,' Nick says, his muted tone matching the gloomy interior of the hotel.

'If he's in here at all,' Dave says, his eyes tracking all parts of the room.

Back in the lobby we realise there are two more corridors leading off from the ground floor, plus the ballroom that I assume leads into the kitchens and back room areas.

'Shall we split up?' Cookey says.

'No mate, it's almost dark now, it'll be pitch black in a minute and we'll end up shooting each other,' I reply, 'we'll stick together, let's try upstairs.'

'The hairs on the back of my neck are standing up,' Nick mutters.

'It's fucking creepy,' Blowers adds in confirmation. I feel it too, that something isn't right but we know we have no choice now. We can't risk being out on the street with just axes and limited rounds in the pistols. The shotguns are good but they take vital seconds to re-load between shots and there's only six of us this time and no automatic weapons. Dave takes point and starts leading us up the stairs, his knives already drawn and held one in each hand; the blades reversed and resting against his forearms. Clarence brings up the rear, his axe held ready. We're all tensed and ready, mouths open and heads cocked, listening intently.

Reaching the first floor, Dave pauses and points to the two corridors leading off. One on each side. We wait for a few seconds, listening for any noises.

'We can split into two teams here, check each corridor and meet back in the middle, Dave and Nick you're with me. Clarence you take the other side,' I instruct in a low whisper. They nod back. Clarence moves away with Blowers and Cookey behind him.

'Nick, you stay in the middle, Dave takes point and I'll bring up the rear,' Dave nods and sets off, taking each step carefully. The sun is rapidly going down and the lack of external windows in the corridor makes it very dark already.

'Nick, have you got a torch in your bag?' Dave asks his voice very soft.

'Hang on,' Nick whispers.

'Stay there Nick, I'll do it,' I step forward and open the top of his bag, carefully pulling the shotgun out and handing it over before I start rooting round. I don't want to press the trigger by mistake. My fingers close round a cold metallic object and I pull out a flashlight, small but with a powerful LED light.

'Keep it off unless we hear something and don't shine it in my eyes, or your own....or Mr Howie's,' Dave instructs quietly. The corridor has hotel rooms on both sides, staggered all the way down. The first is on the right. Dave reaches it and pauses, listening before trying the handle. The door opens easily enough and he darts in, Nick waits in the doorway and I keep watch in the corridor, my axe grasped tightly in both hands. We go from room to room, Dave checking each one and leaving the door open once finished. In the last room, Dave enters then emerges almost immediately with a look of alarm on his face.

'Back to the middle quick,' he mutters urgently. We jog back to find Clarence and the other two coming out of their corridor.

'Did you see them?' Clarence asks with concern.

'I did, look down there,' Dave replies pointing out of the window down to the street.

'He's fucking trapped us,' I say in shock at the sight of zombies shuffling across the road towards the hotel.

'There's fucking loads of them,' Blowers says through gritted teeth.

'Shit...here they go,' I murmur needlessly. We can all see they've frozen on the spot with heads turned up to the now darkened sky. The howling splits the night air and we freeze as the unmistakeable sound is echoed from deep within the hotel. There are several of them by the sounds of it, but the noises from outside and the old fashioned layout of the building make it impossible to pinpoint the exact direction of the sounds. My heart rate increases and I feel a surge of adrenalin coursing through me; that all too familiar sensation I get before a fight commences. Staring back outside I see Darren standing in the road roaring into the air, he stops and looks up at us. Without thinking I draw my pistol and fire through the window, just missing as he ducks down out of sight. I know what I've done as soon as I pull the trigger.

'Fuck it, I'm so sorry,' I apologise, knowing the shot will bring them all in our direction.

'Forget it, I was going for mine too,' Clarence rumbles.

'Me too,' Nick adds.

'My fault for leading you in here,' Dave says flatly.

'You didn't, I did, and you said he could have gone over the wall or round the other side,' I reply. All of us try to make each other feel better.

'Well, I blame Cookey,' Blowers says, I can't help but chuckle quietly.

'Cookey, this is your fault,' I say to him.

'Sorry Mr Howie, it won't happen again,' Cookey replies quickly.

'Yes well I am making a note of it for your yearly appraisal,' I say in a mock officious tone, 'well I guess we'd better find somewhere to hold up.'

'Top floor?, at least we get a nice view then' Clarence suggests.

'Why not, top floor it is.' Dave takes point and we follow him up the spiral staircase. Going slower now because of the dark. Bangs and scrapes sound out all over the building and my already strained nerves are straining even more than normal.

Second floor and Dave pauses, staring hard at the entrance to the darkened corridor. Just before I hear the fast footsteps he's already away, running to the entrance and stepping to the side just as a naked undead comes flying out of the shadows, his teeth already bared. Dave steps up behind him and slices through his neck with ease. The undead goes down noisily, crashing down the stairs and tumbling to the floor below.

'Stop staring at his arse Cookey,' Blowers remarks as the almost decapitated corpse tumbles past them.

We follow Dave up the stairs, going faster now. Clarence at the back. I hear footsteps and a low growl and turn to see an undead running up the stairs at us. Clarence holds for a second then steps in, sweeping his axe round and driving the undead over the low wall and crashing down into the chandelier on the ground level. I lean over and catch a glimpse of many figures running across the lobby towards the base of the stairs. The moonlight shining on their pale skin.

'Fucking shift it, loads of them coming,' I say loudly. Dave increases his pace with us following in his wake. We reach the third floor landing as an undead comes out of the corridor, Dave doesn't even break his stride. Lashing out with one blade to sever through the throat and kicking the zombie back down the corridor. A dark spray of blood arcs into the air as he falls.

'I'm not built for running,' Clarence rumbles behind me, his breathing sounding laboured.

'Almost there,' Dave calls back.

At the top I can see the landing is well illuminated from the unobstructed moon shining through the windows.

'Hold here, Blowers and Cookey you take the left corridor. Nick and Dave take the right. Clarence; you and me will take the top of the stairs.' They shout affirmations back at me.

'Use the shotguns down the corridor, one fires and one loads,' Dave calls out, heading over to his corridor entrance with Nick. I drop my bag on the floor quickly pulling the shotgun and cartridges out while Clarence covers me. I finish and take over, holding central position and listening to them thundering up the stairs. Low growls, groans and snarls rise up ahead of them adding to the already terrifying atmosphere.

'CONTACT,' Blowers shouts before unloading both barrels down the corridor, the sound is immense and booms out into the quiet building.

The first undead turns the corner of the curved staircase, his rotting face glinting in the pale moonlight. He snarls and bursts towards me with a fresh surge of energy then loses his head as I swing out and take him clean through the neck. I shove out with my foot and send his cadaver thumping down the stairs, his body crashing into the undead following in his wake, knocking them flying to both sides like bowling pins. Clarence joins me and I move over so we have an equal share at the top of the staircase. Shots indicate they're attacking in the corridors at the same time as the staircase. More reach the top and Clarence and I both swing out, striking into them and chopping through their bones like a hot knife through butter. Our axes almost clash as we swing, the long handles proving to be unwieldy for two men standing so close together.

'KEEP GOING,' stepping back I shout at Clarence, he shifts position to stand in the centre, already making use of the increased space and taking wider swings with his axe. I drop my axe and take up both shotguns. Leaning over the banister I point the shotguns, one in each hand down at the staircase. Four shots is all I have and I take them quickly, each one booming out in quick succession.

The effect is awesome, the reduced length of the barrel means the pellets spread out quickly and from this range the zombies are cut to pieces. Firing down onto them also means the pellets strike their heads first, exploding skulls and smashing brains apart. The bodies fall back down the stairs, straight into the path of the zombies still coming up. They stagger over their fallen undead while I drop down and break each gun to re-load the four barrels, snapping them back together and leaning over to fire again.

A few get through and are quickly sent packing by Clarence's almighty swings. I glance up while reloading and see him take a massive upper cut, driving the blade into the groin and nearly split-ting the body in half through to the shoulders, he roars as he pulls the axe back out and swings again. Steady shots from both sides of me indicate they are getting multiple contacts from the corridors too

'There's too many,' Blowers shouts loudly. I stand up, snapping both my guns shut and run towards them, diving down to stretch both hands through the gap between their legs. I unload the four barrels down the corridor and see the thick oncoming horde being blasted backwards. I shuffle out and move back to the bags, re-loading the shotguns as fast as my hands will allow.

'Dave are you clear down there?' I shout over.

'We can be do you want it cleared?' He yells back.

'The other corridors thick with 'em, we need to move out.'

'Got it, hold your fire Nick.' Glancing up I see Dave drop his shotgun and draw his knives before running into the corridor. Thumps and bangs mark his progress as he slaughters undead with graceful ease. Nick stands there holding his shotgun, his mouth hanging open.

'Nick, support the other side,' I shout, he snaps to attention and runs over to help Blowers and Cookey. I lean over the wall just in time to see the stairs are thick with undead and Clarence struggling to hold them from gaining the top. I unload the barrels into them and watch with satisfaction as many are blown away, but it's not enough and they are quickly replaced with more growling snarling beasts.

'DAVE ARE YOU CLEAR?' I shout.

'CLEAR,' he yells back.

'FALL BACK TO DAVE'S CORRIDOR.' I shout, after re-loading both shotguns. Clarence turns and scoops up both our bags then, brandishing the axe with one hand, he takes another mighty sweep through the heads of the front row of zombies, cleaving their skulls open. I drop back to the corridor and turn to face out.

'NOW,' I bellow. Blowers, Cookey and Nick all turn to run past me. Clarence roars as he takes another sweep then quickly backs away, going into the corridor. I aim one shotgun at the staircase and the other at the mouth of the other corridor. Pausing just long enough for them to come through. I fire both guns with both barrels and snarl with satisfaction as I see them blown backwards.

'FALL BACK,' Dave shouts behind me. I move into the corridor and run down a few metres. Clarence is now at the front, giving protection from anything coming up. Dave fires his shotgun, one barrel in each direction. Blowers steps in front of him and repeats the action, followed by Nick and Cookey.

'FIND A CLEAR ROOM,' Dave yells. I've just re-loaded both my guns and I push the closest door open. Luckily the door swings straight into the male zombie standing behind it, causing him to stagger back slightly. I fire one barrel into his face and pull the door closed before moving down the corridor to try the next one. This time I kick the door open and see two undead inside. They get the remaining three barrels and the faded floral wallpaper is freshly layered with zombie gore. The door is pulled closed and I drop down to quickly re-load the shotguns. Clarence roars and I glance up to see him standing at the end of the corridor, chopping undead down as they surge from another staircase. Constant shots from the other end tell me they're still busy too. With both guns re-loaded I try the next door. Nothing apparent so I enter the large room. An old bed frame, side cabinets and a dressing table. Two doors in the wall. I kick the first one open and step back, bathroom; all clear. The second door leads to an adjoining room. Also clear. I head back to the corridor and deliver the news at the top of my voice.

'COVER ME,' Clarence shouts. I move in his direction while he backs towards me. We pass each other and I fire two barrels at the advancing undead while moving backwards. Dave orders the others to drop back while he covers them. Blowers, Cookey and Nick move down the corridor and enter the room. I pause in the doorway watching Clarence run into the adjoining room and lug the old bed frame across to the external door, wedging it tight. A quick check down the corridor reveals more undead coming towards me. I fire down at them and remember Chris's words about how devastating these weapons are at close range.

'CLEAR,' Clarence shouts.

'DAVE FALL BACK,' I yell out as Nick joins me in the corridor, firing his now re-loaded shotgun into the horde. Dave drops back quickly and chucks his shotgun into the room before shoving a flash-light into his mouth and drawing his knives. He runs back up the corridor before I can say anything and commences a thirty second killing spree, the torch light dancing about as he spins, drops and leaps in the darkened corridor. Blowers and Cookey step out, see Dave and turn to fire their weapons down the corridor. The light dances down towards us as Dave runs back, removing the flashlight from his mouth as he enters the room.

'Better now?' I ask him pointedly.

'Much better thank you,' he smiles back at me as Blowers slams the door shut. We quickly push the old furniture against the door. Me, Dave and Nick in this room and the other three in the adjoining room. We all step back at the same time, staring at each other through the connecting door, chests heaving and smiling like idiots.

'Fuck me, that was intense,' Blowers mutters.

'We're in a hotel, not tents,' Nick quips back.

'Very funny captain Blackbeard, what now?' Blowers asks.

'Eat, drink and be merry,' Clarence calls from the other room, 'for tonight we fight,' he makes his voice even deeper than normal, sounding like a Hollywood voice over man. The guns are re-loaded quickly, and we take the opportunity to do as Clarence jokingly suggested. We drink water and eat food taken from the stores back in the fort and use anti-bacterial wet wipes to clean ourselves down. Thumps and bangs come from behind both doors but the furniture is wedged in tight and it will take them a while to beat their way through.

'Nice view,' Cookey remarks, finding the balcony door and looking down the hill at the sea.

'Have you seen more naked men?' Blowers asks.

'Fuck you Blowers, but shit...take a look at that lot.' We join him out on the balcony and look down to see the hotel is surrounded by thick crowds of zombies.

'Stitched up like a kipper,' I mutter.

'What?' Dave asks.

'It's a saying,' I answer him.

'Oh, do kippers get stitched up then?'

'I don't know, do they?' I ask to shakes of heads and shrugs of shoulders. Looking down the hill I can see the inky black of the water, but where this would have once been clearly defined by the lights of the mainland, it's now completely black. The only lights are the flashing green and red buoys in the sea. Staring down at the zombies surrounding us, a thought process forms in my mind.

'They must be locked out,' the others look at me, 'this hotel is huge and they could easily fit inside.'

'Good spot,' Clarence says, 'that means we've got a finite amount in here with us.'

'If I'm right,' I reply quickly.

'I think you are,' Dave says, 'they're not going anywhere, just waiting,' he nods down at the ground as he speaks.

'So Smithy did trap us then,' Nick says, giving voice to all our thoughts, 'he put them zombies in the rooms, led us up here, let more in and then shut the doors so we can't get out.'

'Clever fucker,' I murmur, 'I bet he's nearby watching.'

'Or he's done it to buy time so he can find our group before we do,' Dave adds.

'If we've got no idea where they went, how will he know?' Cookey asks.

'But if he's got control over the other zombies, couldn't he tap into what they've seen or heard? Maybe some of them saw our group moving about,' Nick says.

'Why set the trap for us then, if he knew where they were? He could have taken this lot and gone straight for them, like he did with us in the fort,' I say.

'So he set the trap for us to buy himself time to find them?' Nick asks.

'Most likely,' Dave answers and coming from him we accept the glimmer of hope that Darren hasn't figured out where they are yet.

'Options? We fight our way out, but that means taking on that lot in the corridor and then those outside, and any others we find on the streets. Or we try and sit it out for a few hours.'

'I think we should wait Mr Howie,' Dave says firmly, 'If Darren knew where they were then he wouldn't have set this trap. He would have gone for them straight awayand not wasted resources by throwing this lot against us. We could fight our way out easily enough but then we'd be running and fighting all night.'

'Everyone agreed?' Nods all round, 'right, we'll do that. Sit and rest until either those doors give or daylight comes...whichever is sooner.

CHAPTER TEN

This feels wonderful. Completely wonderful. The world has gone to rat shit and everyone is either turned into a zombie or is hiding away with their heads under the bed sheets. Not me though. Not now. I can walk these streets with impunity. Nothing can touch me now. I've no doubt that Howie and that cuntrunt Dave could fight their way out of the hotel, but that would leave them stranded on the streets in a strange place with no idea where to go and the area crawling with my charged up lovelies. No, they'll stay there, tucked up safe and sound. Buying me a few hours of darkness to figure out where those fucking piggies went. Walking along a side street I come out into the town centre, another steep hill but this one full of shops and pubs. The pier is at the bottom of this street and the whole area is covered with bodies. Stacks of bodies. There's loads of pubs here so I figure that the town must have been packed when it all started. Seeing the bodies rotting on the street makes me tut, what a waste of perfectly good bodies that I could have used.

The smell of death is different to that of my brothers and sisters. Sure, they smell rotten and rancid, but not dead. The difference is clearly distinct. Still, the stench doesn't bother me, it's quite nice really. The weather is warm, Howie and his cunts are having a stressful time and I'm wandering the streets hunting for his little bumchums.

Thanks to fuckwit Howie giving the game away, I can safely assume he did send them over here. The speed in which they got over the water tells me they're worried. But also that they don't know where they went either. Otherwise they wouldn't be charging around after me and stopping to have a scrap. So they don't know where they went and I don't know where they went, so where did they go? There must have been quite a few of them so they would need somewhere big enough to hide away. Why doesn't Howie know where they are though? He must have figured we'd get the information if we caught them, or tap into their cerebral knowledge with our amazing zombie powers. Fuck I wish I had those powers back. That old boy was connected to me, it must have been because I bit him. I need to find some more survivors so I can bite them and have them under my control too.

The cellar under the hotel, that's full of stupid panicking survivors. But all my babies are busy and it would mean doing it all myself. Still, it's only just got dark and I've got a few hours to kill, Ha hours to kill! I make myself laugh. Fucking cunts, hiding away while I'm up here doing all the work, struggling and for what? What I ask you? For nothing. That's what. Fucking wankers, they deserve to die. Sitting down there eating shit and drinking piss and making that old man come out on his own. Fucking cowards, I saw them throw him out. Poor old boy was terrified too. Yeah, they should suffer. There's a big pub here with large plate glass windows. One of them modern things that doesn't play music but where everyone sits down pretending to be smart and clever. Fuckwits, fucking fuckwits.

I wish they were here now so I could rip their faces off with my teeth. Behind the bar I grab a couple of bottles of spirits and head back down the road, stopping to tear a strip of some already half naked dead woman reveller. Fucking slut, running around with her tits bouncing about and flashing her thong about. Yeah not so hot now are you, I spit on her face to show my distaste for her choice of skimpy clothing. The spittle lands obscenely on her cheek and starts sliding down. The material won't tear and I get frustrated, kicking her in her already decomposing stomach. The skin rips apart and covers my shoes in her filthy stinking innards.

'Fucking whore,' I spit down again and wipe my dirty shoes on her face and hair. The next corpse yields his top easily enough as I yank it from him and set off back down the street towards the seafront.

At the bottom a sign for a shop catches my eye and makes me turn back. A newsagents and convenience store, with a sign advertising local guide books. I scoot over and find it's already been well looted with crap and debris all over the floor.

'Messy fuckers,' I tut again as I work my way to the back where the magazines are displayed. I see the thick fucking looters didn't take any reading material with them.

'That's the problem with this country, distinct lack of education,' I mutter to myself as I root through the shitty little pamphlets, 'I blame the parents myself, aah what's this, what's this?' I pick up a local guide book and start flicking though but it's too dark for even my super charged wonderfully infected lovely red bloodshot zombie eyes to read.

Outside in the moonlight I flick through the pages as I walk along the promenade and back towards the hotel with the cellar full of my supper. The stupid fucking book is full of wanky adverts, telling me where to eat and what shop to get my clothes from, telling me I can get two meals for the price of one on Tuesdays between 2pm and 2.05pm. Fucking cunts, that's what ruined this world. Stupid fucking adverts written by stupid fuckwits, and education of course. No wonder we had to take over. Saving the world is what we're doing really. Fuck, it would be ruined if left to these stupid cheese eaters, blowing each other up and boring everyone to death. Look at it now, it's Saturday night on a mid-summer evening and I'm in a holiday town filled with pubs and not a fight in sight. Much better. Mrs

Miggins could safely walk her dog through here, well if she was a zombie walking a zombie dog she could anyway.

Can dogs get infected? Fuck it; I'll try it when I find one. I hate dogs, nasty fucking things with big teeth showing off because they can piss up things and shit where they want.

Reaching the railing I tuck the tour guide into my waistband and stare down at the cellar door before easing the gate open and sneaking down the stairs. I empty both bottles of spirits onto the ground and slink back up a few steps, stopping to soak the material in the liquid. At the top, I move round so I'm closer to the main door and light the material with the lighter I sourced earlier. It flames instantly so I drop it over the railings and watch as the flammable liquid ignites. Chuckling to myself I run up the stairs and back through the hotel door, working my way back through the corridor towards the other cellar door.

It's pitch black in here but that suits me perfectly. I find the door and wait for a few seconds until I hear the low murmurs, then the raised voices and finally the panicked screams and shouts as they realise one of their exits is on fire. The place must be full of smoke already because I can hear loads of coughing coming from down there. They're arguing and trying to figure out what they should do, someone shouts to get out; someone else shouts it could be a trap, the first one shouts it doesn't matter if they all get burnt to death. That seems to do the trick and the next noise is people thundering up the stairs towards the door I'm standing behind.

The door swings open and the first one staggers out coughing hard, smoke is pouring out of the cellar which is wonderful as it will mask my presence and make it more confusing. I slip out from behind the door and my eyes pick up the silhouette of a figure bent over and coughing hard. I slip in behind them and ease them away.

'Come on quick,' I say with pretend concern. The figure, a woman by the feel of the fleshy mounds hanging down from inside her top, responds easily enough and lets me lead her away a few metres. I clamp my hand over her mouth nice and hard and take a chunk out of the back of her neck, tearing the flesh apart and sucking on the blood. She squirms and tries to fight but it only takes seconds before she slumps down to the ground.

I go back towards the door and find someone else staggering about blindly and coughing, the trick works again and I lead this one a few meters until he trips over the body on the floor and falls down. I land on top of him, scrabbling to cover his mouth while I gnash my teeth into his stomach. I bite down and savage through the flesh, he screams loudly and I hear more people running my way. I jump and shout, 'quick, he's fallen over,' they come running in and everything erupts into sweet bedlam with me tearing at their flesh and dragging them down onto the floor. The smoke, their eyes stinging and watering and the almost pitch black of the corridor makes it impossible for them to see and I take full advantage of it.

It's over in minutes, a few escaped but I bit a couple of those that ran off so I know they'll turn soon. Leaving my bodies in the corridor I descend the stairs into the cellar and find it's a disused bar, like a speakeasy from the movies. Wooden bar, wooden tables and wooden chairs and even old beer mats on the bar top. Signs of the survivors are everywhere with stacks of tinned food, bottles of water and buckets overflowing with shit and piss. Dirty fuckers, how can they live like this? I've done them a favour really; bringing them over to my side. Better than living in this filth.

The fire has taken hold over by the door and the whole place is filled with thick smoke. Good job I'm not living otherwise this would kill me, but even in my dead state I find it choking.

A whimper makes me turn and head behind the bar to find a body tucked up in the foetal position. Must have crawled in here to die, rather than face the terror outside. The body whimpers again, long curly black hair covering a face and the gentle curves of a womanly form. I gently push the hair away and see a beautiful face, soft red lips and dark eyes framed by arching black eyebrows. Stunning woman, beautiful really and I gaze down at her for a few minutes until I realise the smoke and flames will over-power even me if I'm not careful. She's alive, barely and I'm captivated by her exquisite beauty. I can't leave her here to die, no way. She's coming with me. I scoop her up in my arms, carry her out from behind the bar and up the stairs back into the darkened corridor. My new converts are waking up, groaning and mumbling away like the hungry little blighters they are.

Carrying the woman I go back through the corridors and out the front door. The escaping survivors came this way too, I can smell them. Once outside I can see thick smoke billowing up from the cellar. I carry the woman to the wide pavement and gently lay her down on the ground. She makes small noises in her throat as I smooth her hair back and stroke her gorgeous face. She's dressed in a filthy white blouse and black skirt; she must have been waitressing in the hotel when it happened.

My undead heart hammers in my infected chest at the sight of her and the thought that I can bite this wonderful creature and take her blood. The newly undead circle around me, clearly sensing she's still human but I growl up at them, marking my territory and they cower back. I can feel a connection with them which confirms what happened with the old boy. It seems I can keep what I bite, and biting this woman fills me with a sensual excitement. Surely nothing can be more intimate than sharing my blood with her so she can turn and join me.

I lean down and hover over her skin, the smell of stale body odour, piss and shit is like perfume to me and I hold off biting her, drawing the torture out like I did with the old man, but this is way more torturous and exciting. My lips brush the side of her neck, then her cheek and her ear. I move down to her bare arms and feel the rush inside me. I don't want to mark her, she's too beautiful.

With loving care I roll her onto her front and unzip the back of her skirt, the action just excites me even more and it gets worse when I tug her skirt down to reveal her perfect tanned bottom. Oh the smell of shit is strong here, so strong and the sight of her firm cheeks makes my mouth drool until strands of saliva are spooling down to glide down her skin and soak into her panties. My tongue darts out to lick her skin, it's too much and I can't hold back anymore. She comes to as I bite down, not too hard but enough to break the skin and feel her beautiful blood flow into my mouth. Her back arches and her hands claw at the pavement. I know it hurts my beauty but it'll be over soon I promise. I bite down harder, unable to contain myself. The urge to burrow my head into her soft arse cheeks is so powerful, I want to eat her all up and have her inside me all the time. But I force myself to pull back, my head spins from the satisfaction and I lie on my back staring at the stars in an almost post coital ecstasy.

Raising my head I look over at the massive flames now licking up from the basement, the cellar must be completely alight now.

'Oops,' I giggle quietly, 'sorry about your hotel.' I look over and realise my beauty is still lying there showing her arse off to the world and my hungry babies are edging closer.

'Fuck off you dirty cunts,' I snarl at them, 'dirty nasty fucking cunts,' I'm on my feet beating them about the head. They cower back, groaning softly as they're beaten by their master. Yeah, I'm their master now. Fuck you Howie; you're not the only one with groupies. I drop down so I'm almost squatting on the backs of her thighs, staring down at her lovely arse and the rapidly congealing wound.

Small rivers of blood run sexily down her skin and I can't help but drop down and lick at them, letting the metallic taste soak into my tongue. Pulling my head down I gently run my fingers over the unbitten arse cheek, feeling the soft warmth and by degrees I increase the pressure until I'm kneading the flesh, taking a big handful and squeezing until she whimpers again.

She suddenly comes to, flipping over onto her back and crabbing backwards. Her eyes are wide and fearful, she glances up at the zombies standing nearby and lets out a scream.

'Oh my god!' she covers her mouth with her hand, glancing quickly between the zombies and me. She scuttles backwards until she's a few metres away, wincing as her wounded arse cheek touches the ground. She reaches down to feel and her hand comes away covered in blood. She keeps staring at the zombies and her breathing is hard and fast like she's hyperventilating.

'Did you know them?' I ask softly. She doesn't answer, just stares at me, tears streaming down her face.

'It won't take long,' I whisper to her. She looks terrified, truly terrified and I almost feel sorry for putting her through this, but know she'll feel better in a few minutes.

'Am I....Am I...?' She stammers between breaths.

'Yes, you're bitten. It won't take long. Just try and relax.' She sobs hard, pitiful cries coming from her very soul. She scrabbles to her feet, holding the falling skirt up.

'No...No...Please...' She starts to back away.

'It's too late,' I follow after her as she tries to run, limping and wincing with pain from her bitten bum

'Please...No....,' she tries to run faster but the infection is taking hold and she falls down onto the ground. I run to her side and try to cradle her in my arms. She fights back, screaming and beating at me with her fists.

'No...please...no...' Her thrashing becomes feebler with every passing second until she gives up and lies still in my arms. Her eyes dart about as her breathing becomes more laboured.

'It's okay, it'll be okay...just go with it,' I stroke her hair and speak softly, her dark eyes look up at me.

'Does it hurt?' She whispers as she grips my arm.

'No, it doesn't hurt. It feels wonderful, amazing. It's the best feeling ever.' She starting to slip now, fighting to stay awake and I can see she's desperately clinging onto life and truly terrified of going under.

'Just relax, don't fight it. It'll be over in seconds.' She stares back me, clearly delirious but her words strike a chord in my heart.

'Promise?'

'I promise.'

'Stay with me...' her voice is barely a whisper. I remember how utterly terrified I was when they pulled me down in London. The thought of dying alone was unbearable and I too gripped at the zombie bodies and pulled them close, desperate for any action of embrace or words of comfort to ease my passing.

With a final spasm she passes away. Her dying breath eases out of her lips and she goes limp. I stroke her head as the flames grow ever bigger behind me, illuminating her in a soft orange glow. Minutes pass and I caress her soft face, so beautiful in death. Then it comes; she jerks slightly and goes still. Jerks again and a spasm runs through her body like an electric current. She opens her eyes and stares straight up at me as I carry on stroking her face. Her eyes are red and bloodshot and the effect just makes her look even more sultry and stunning.

'I promised it wouldn't hurt didn't I?' Stroking her soft face I look down at the newest member of my horde. Her eyes fix on mine, her head not lolling and her body no longer twitching with spasmodic jerks.

'Yes you did,' she replies.

CHAPTER ELEVEN

They break though after a few hours, finally forcing the door open and using sheer body weight to push the barrier towards us.

'They've given up on this one,' Clarence calls, running into our room.

'They're all pushing on this side,' I reply handing Clarence his shotgun.

'Keep it; I'll stick with the axe.'

'Fair enough big man.' Walking forward I lean over the barrier and shove the shotgun into the rapidly growing gap where the door is being pushed open. A zombie lunges in and tries biting the end of one of the guns. Four shots later and there's a slight pause as the zombies not blown to bits lurch forward for another attack.

'I fucking love these guns,' I shout as Blowers runs in and takes a shot, followed by Cookey then Nick.

'Save the rounds, there can't be that many left,' Dave says and I suspect he's getting jealous at us racking the kills up with the sawn off weapons.

'We've got loads of cartridges left,' I smile at him.

'Yeah but we don't know what we're going to meet or have to deal with and we might need them.'

'Yeah but there's loads of farms we can break into, and I bet a rural place like this has loads of gunsmiths.'

'Yeah but we don't know if anyone has already been and taken them.'

'Yeah but it's fun....I like sawn off shotguns,' he realises I'm pissing about and chooses to ignore me, focussing on the barrier slowly giving way and the increasing groans coming from the undead forcing their way in.

The barrier finally collapses. The first couple of undead trip over the furniture and land heavily but the rest surge through. Dave leaps into the fray before the rest of us have a chance to react. Knives drawn he sets about them with his amazing agility. Clarence moves forward and stands nearby with his axe, but every time he goes to swipe at one, Dave nips in and takes it down. The rest of us stand and watch, mesmerised by Dave. He holds a central position, letting them come to him but the way he flexes, stretches, drops down and pivots is extraordinary. I've lost count of the amount of times I've seen this but it never ceases to amaze me and I don't think it ever will. A noise to my side, Nick lighting a cigarette, he shrugs at me and I shrug back. Watching them it's almost comical. The huge figure of Clarence wielding a double bladed axe and constantly trying to dart forward and the much smaller figure of Dave, slaughtering them with pathetic ease. Dave feints to the side and one slips past him only to be sliced in half by Clarence taking his frustration out with a powerful swing.

The bodies stack up on the floor, creating another barrier to the rest outside. Dave steps back for a rest while we watch the undead try to climb the bloody corpses and slip back down into the corridor.

'You missed one,' Clarence states, very matter of fact.

'I let him through for you.'

'You missed him.'

'I knew you were there so I let him through.'

'I don't need your charity,' Clarence growls.

'You were getting frustrated so I let you have one.'

'You let me have one?' Clarence steps closer to Dave, staring down at the little man.

'Anger is an enemy and frustration causes mistakes,' Dave replies, unflinching beneath the big man's intense gaze.

'What...did you say?' Clarence goes bright red and I see his already huge arm muscles bulge as he tenses up.

'Calm down, there's plenty left,' Dave's tone strikes a chord and Clarence throws the axe down on the floor. Fuck me, the biggest man I've ever seen is about to have a fight with the most dangerous man I've ever seen. Nick and the other two keep glancing at me in alarm.

'Lads...take it easy,' I adopt a friendly tone. They completely ignore me and stand with eyes locked. There can't be many men that can stare Clarence down but Dave tries, maybe not even realising what he's doing.

Clarence turns with incredible speed and pulls the barrier out of the way then kicks at the stacked up corpses, sending them flying into the undead behind them. He roars and leaps over them and straight into the zombies, his fists flying out and battering them with savage brutality. Dave turns and watches, his face completely devoid of expression. Clarence rages, roaring with anger as he lashes out. Punching with a staggering ferocity, he lashes backwards with his elbow, breaking the neck of an undead about to lunge at him from behind. He bends down and scoops up a body then starts using it like a battering ram, swatting the other zombies with the corpse. His strong legs strike down as he stamps on heads, crushing skulls. Seconds later it's over, Clarence scans the corridor and seemingly satisfied he drops the body and steps back into the room.

'Fuck me, we might as well go home,' Cookey mutters quietly.

'You alright mate?' I drop back and speak quietly to Clarence, hopefully out of ear shot of Dave at the front taking point as we make our way back down the stairs, carefully stepping over the bodies of the zombies we killed earlier.

'Fine,' one word answer and I sense the brooding mood he's in.

'Dave takes some getting used to, but he's a good bloke.'

'Okay.' The tone is softer, relenting a little and I leave it at that, any more from me would risk being patronising to this highly trained soldier.

The shotgun is now back in my bag, reluctantly put away so I can use the quieter axe if we find opposition. We make our way back down to the lobby and crouch down in the shadows watching the silhouetted figures of the zombies outside.

'Rest here, the sun will be up soon and we can move out,' I whisper quietly to Blowers, he repeats the instruction down the line until I see Dave nod back at me, then crouch down to rest his back against the wall.

CHAPTER TWELVE

'You can speak?'

'Yes!' She looks up at me as I cradle her in my arms, and the only sign of the infection is the red eyes. My zombie mind whirls and spins and I almost drop her in surprise.

'You were right, it feels fantastic,' she purrs and snuggles her body closer to me, 'the pain has gone and I feel all warm inside. Warm and tingly.' She lets out a low moan and I can't help but stare at her.

'Although, if I am honest I do feel a little hungry, very hungry in fact,' her voice is soft and velvety, deep and sensual.

'Are you okay?' She smiles up at me with straight white teeth her pink tongue darting out to moisten her full red lips.

'How can you speak?' I ask and my tone is hard.

'Can't you all speak?' She purrs.

'You know they can't speak...I'm the only one.'

'You can't be the only one...' She teases, tilting her face down and looking up at me through dark eyelashes.

'I thought I was. But now there's you,' her eyes lock on mine and I lose myself in their beauty, feeling her warm dead body pressing close to mine. The hotel fire rages behind us. The light of the flames dancing across the road surface and glinting off the smashed up cars. Fragments of broken car window scatter the ground; catching the light, dazzling and intoxicating. My lovelies gather round us, me and this beautiful zombie woman speaking so softly to me. My mind races as I try to think of how this has happened, how she can speak, why she is different like me. So many questions, so many things to think about but for now I can't take my eyes off her.

A chemistry ignites sparks between us, my zombie heart pounds as she grips my shoulders to lift herself up closer to my face. I lean down until we're just inches apart, eyes locked. I want to kiss her, I want to bite her and taste her blood again. She feels the same, her lips pull back and make ready for the bite but then press together readying for the kiss. We pucker and snarl as the conflicting urges surge through us...bite....kiss...tear...caress. Our lips gently brush, so soft. Her grip intensifies on my shoulders as she bares her teeth and growls at me. I show mine and snarl back at her, our lips constantly touch and break apart. My mouth brushes her warm cheek, her grip softens and I move down to gently brush against her neck. She stretches sensually as I nuzzle at her skin. Sensations sweep through me and I push my head down, she stretches harder as my teeth push down on the taught flesh. She groans and pulls me in, longing for me to bite her. She nestles round and pushes her mouth against my neck, gently kissing, electric tingles run up and down my spine. Her kissing gets firmer, harder. Teeth against my skin, a low groan escapes my throat as the pressure gets stronger. Her tongue flicks out, licking me. My head swims as she bites again, her teeth pushing in. My hand goes to the back of her head, pulling her closer. She responds and bites harder as I push her head against me, my fingers entwine in her soft hair. Her arms, wrapped around my shoulders tighten, and she bites down. I feel my skin tear as she pierces the flesh and her tongue licks at my infected blood. She groans louder and sucks my neck, drawing more blood into her mouth. The pain is ecstasy, pure ecstasy and like nothing I have ever felt before.

My hands drop down to lift her bodily onto my lap, she straddles me. Her thighs wrap around my stomach as she licks and sucks hungrily at my neck. I drop my hand down and feel the firmness of her arse cheeks and her skirt rides up. Kneading and caressing, my hand touches the wound and she flinches.

'Sorry,' I whisper into her ear.

'Touch it,' she groans back at me. My hand moves round, slowly sweeping the curve of her rounded butt. Fingers brush against bare skin, probing, touching, feeling for the wound. She groans and licks at my neck. The tips of my fingers brush the wound, she pushes into me with whimpers of pleasure.

'Touch it,' she says again. My fingers gently stroke the torn flesh going back and forth and she presses her body against mine.

'Again,' she pleads. My fingers brush over the ragged wound, applying more pressure. Her body tenses and she moans.

'Harder,' she begs, I respond and rub with force. She pushes into me, her body pulsating, thrusting, rocking.

'Harder,' she commands. My hand grips and squeezes at the laceration. Her mouth locks onto my neck, sucking and licking. Her hot tongue probes my bitten flesh, easing the blood out. I feel the liquid drip down my neck, sending more shivers though me.

The ecstasy builds as we thrust our bodies into each other. My hand roughly explores the moist, sticky hole in her arse. She pulls the collar of my shirt away from my neck, exposing my shoulder. She grips me with all her strength and buries her mouth onto my flesh, biting down, tearing at it. My body is on fire as the pressure builds. I move my free hand round to rub at her while I lift the first bloodied hand to my mouth, licking at the blood. She pulls away from my shoulder, hungrily sucks on my fingers, tasting her own blood. Eyes lock. Chests heave as we pant, push eager fingers into open wounds, taste blood. There is only now, this moment. Our minds are as mingled and entwined as our blood. The pressure releases, our bodies are taut, straining with orgasm. Shuddering, shaking and groaning with pure pleasure.

I have no idea how long we are locked together. Seconds that seeml like eternity. We lie on the road, side by side, bodies entwined. Watching the hotel burn.

'It's beautiful,' she says softly.

'What is?'

'The fire, the power of it; it's beautiful.'

'It is.'

'Can it hurt us?' Rolling onto her side, she faces me as she asks the question.

'Yes, anything can hurt us just the same as before. But we don't feel pain like we used to. Our injuries heal a lot faster, our blood clots quicker and it takes more to kill us.'

'What does kill us?'

'They'll go for the head mainly, or a massive attack to the body. Like chopping legs off or splitting the stomach open.'

'Who? Who's they?'

'Survivors... Howie and his lot,' I spit the words out with venom.

'Howie?'

'He's a fucking wanker, him and his cuntrunt mate Dave.'

'Who are they?' She asks me. We lie together as I recount the journey, the story, the history of what happened, who they all are and why I'm here. My tale of woe takes a time to tell but she listens intently. Squeezing my hand at the sad times, like when Howie abused me so badly on the bridge and laughing at the good times, like when I killed Jamie and the old couple in the shop. It feels good to talk and I realise how much I've missed being able to communicate like this. This makes me think again about why she's different.

'I don't know,' she answers when I put the question to her, 'I woke up to find you groping my arse you dirty man,' she laughs, ' I remember the fear I felt at being bitten, and recognising them too,' she motions to the other zombies still gathered round us. 'I remember going under and being terrified but then I was back and it felt differ-ent, completely different. Is that how it was for you?'

'Exactly the same. They pinned me down and I was shitting myself but then I came back. But it was different. There were thousands and thousands of them and I controlled all of them. I could feel their connection in my mind and make them do what I wanted. As we came down from London to the fort I could sense more of them joining us. Oh you should have seen it. Our brothers and sisters as far as the eye could see.'

'And you controlled all of them?'

'Every single one, but I was the only one that could speak or think like this, or so I thought.'

'You're special, unique, powerful,' she purrs the words, caressing my arm.

'And now you're here,' I turn to face her, 'and I wonder what for?'

'I don't know...to help you. To help you stop that Howie and his nasty friends.'

'Is that why?' My gaze locks on her face.

'Why else?'

'Maybe you want to be in charge, maybe I've failed and now you've been selected to take over,' my voice grows harder as I speak. 'Yeah, I've failed and I'm not needed, yeah Smithy just fuck off and let someone else have a go eh? Going to take over are you? Come here to kill me have you?' I'm on my feet, raging and shouting at her. She looks alarmed and stands up, staring at me with her beautiful eyes.

'Yeah, trying to seduce me with your....your...your arse! Thrusting your tits at me and making me have zombie sex with you.'

'We didn't have sex...'

'Well, whatever we did, it felt like sex.'

'It was amazing, you were amazing...'

'That's not the point, don't try and woo me over with your womanly charms. Oh no, coming here to take me over and make me a slave like one of them,' I point to the nearest zombie which drools away as it stares between the woman and I.

'I don't even know your name!' I shout.

'It's Marcy,' she laughs, 'my name is Marcy. What's yours? Smithy did you say?'

'Darren, its Darren Smith. Everyone always called me Smithy.'

'Then I shall call you Darren.'

'Stop putting me off when I'm ranting.'

'Darren my love, it's clear why I'm here,' she walks towards me, stares up through those dark red eyes, 'my purpose is clear my love, I'm here for you, to help you...' I start to protest but she moves in and puts her hand gently to my mouth.

'Why else would you have saved me from the fire, why else would you have bitten me the way you did. You avoided my face and took me in the bum.' I blanch at the expression she uses, she smiles back.

'Sorry, I meant bit me in the bum....you bit my bum, bit it hard and took my blood,' she whispers and I feel the erotic sensation building up again. We stand close, breathing hard and she licks the scabbed blood on my neck.

'Can we have sex?' She asks me softly.

'Now?' I reply, shocked.

'No, I mean can we? Can zombies have sex?' she laughs and the sound is music to my ears. Like the strangulated death gurgle of a human.

'I don't know.' My heart is hammering again.

'Does it work?' she presses in closer, her hand dropping down to my groin, 'oh it works, it works very well.' She pushes and rubs, building the tension.

'Shit,' I exclaim.

'What's wrong?'

'The sun's coming up; we've been here for hours. We need to move.' She pulls back, staring at the sky.

'Follow me, I know where we can hide,' she starts to pull me away.

'Hide? I'm not hiding from any fucker. I'm going after his little piggies,' I argue back.

'Darren, they'll be out soon and they'll come looking for you. That will tell them you were here,' she nods to the blazing building across the road, 'we need to rest, get more bodies and plan smartly.' I bridle at the implication, she senses it.

'Darren my sweet, you've done so well. You're so powerful and strong but I believe I was put here to help you. We can plan together. Howie and his friends think you're going straight after the others and will follow you. They don't realise that you don't know where to find them either.'

'So let's get there first so we can fuck them over.'

'Darren, trust me, please,' she looks into my eyes, and my undead heart melts. I want Howie's piggies to die and suffer. I want that cunt sister of his to suffer the death of a thousand bites but maybe she's right. So far I've been predictable, other than trapping them in the hotel that is. The stupid fucktards, getting trapped by a zombie. Fuck you Howie, I'm not just a zombie, I'm a super zombie.

Dragging my eyes from Marcy's I gaze across the road at the blackened remnants of the burned out hotel then back at the beautiful zombie woman I rescued from it. I don't resist as she takes my hand and starts to pull me down the street.

The latest recruits to our undead army trail loyally in our wake.

ALSO BY RR HAYWOOD

EXTRACTED SERIES

EXTRACTED

EXECUTED

EXTINCT

International best-selling time-travel

#1 Amazon US

#1 Amazon UK

#1 Audible US & UK

Top 3 Amazon Australia

Washington Post Best-seller

In 2061, a young scientist invents a time machine to fix a tragedy in his past. But his good intentions turn catastrophic when an early test reveals something unexpected: the end of the world.

A desperate plan is formed. Recruit three heroes, ordinary humans capable of extraordinary things, and change the future.

Safa Patel is an elite police officer, on duty when Downing Street comes under terrorist attack. As armed men storm through the breach, she dispatches them all.

'Mad' Harry Madden is a legend of the Second World War.

Not only did he complete an impossible mission—to plant charges on a heavily defended submarine base—but he also escaped with his life.

Ben Ryder is just an insurance investigator. But as a young man he witnessed a gang assaulting a woman and her child. He went to their rescue, and killed all five.

Can these three heroes, extracted from their timelines at the point of death, save the world?

Printed in Great Britain
by Amazon